# TUSKERS

## Day of the Long Pig

~ BOOK 2 ~

## by DUNCAN McGEARY

The Jeep was surrounded by pigs. Hairy, ugly pigs.

Donny stopped, and his hand went to the knife at his belt. "Shoo," he said to the animals.

It should have been an enchanting moment, a brush with the local wildlife, but there was something odd in the way the pigs were arrayed: not at random, but almost in ranks. And there was a pig in front that was simply enormous, half again as big as the others.

It grunted, and several of the smaller pigs trotted forward, coming directly at Donny. He pulled out his knife and waved it at them, but they keep coming. Then they were swirling around his legs. Donny stabbed downward, but didn't seem to hit anything; then he let out a cry of pain. Melissa wanted to run to him, but was frozen in fear.

Suddenly, Donny was on his knees. He'd dropped the knife and was clutching his ankles. Blood was welling over the tops of his shoes, soaking the yellowish slate.

The big pig trotted forward, his head now at the same height as Donny's. They seemed to be staring into each other's eyes.

The animal slammed into Donny's midsection, and he slumped over. Something wet and white and visceral sloshed onto the ground in front of him, and he let out a ghastly rattle, as if he was already dead and his last breath was slowly being released.

He toppled over and fell into three parts. The lower part of his body went backward, the top of his torso went forward, and the middle part splashed wetly between them. Melissa saw a look of horror in his unseeing eyes. And then she was screaming and screaming. She must have started running, because she slammed into the rear door of the Jeep. Luckily, they hadn't bothered to lock it, and she scrambled inside.

To my brother, Mike, who—even if he didn't know it—made me try harder.

# Chapter One

They were driving up a dirt road so narrow and steep they had no choice but to keep going. There was no way to back the Jeep down in reverse without one of the tires slipping on the loose shale, lurching over the edge, and pulling them over the cliff.

Melissa looked over at Donny, his jaw clenched but a wild excitement in his eyes. It was crazy, but she had a strange faith in him, in his luck. He was so alive, so vital, so much the artist.

Until she'd met him, she'd thought *she* was an artist. Oh, she had the aesthetic sense, perhaps, but she didn't have Donny's boundless curiosity and daring. The other students were in awe of him. He was older than most of them by a decade but seemed younger in spirit. He had real-world experience as a carpenter and was on a mission to get his master's degree and teach art.

"I want to go where the roads end," he'd said the last time the full class met. "Who wants to go with me?"

When no one else spoke up, Melissa surprised herself by raising her hand. It was her chance to get him alone, soak him up, and crawl over him and into him. To see the world as he saw it; to learn to live again.

Where she saw a featureless desert, he saw an endless plain of wonder.

This vision was what they'd been sent down here to see. When Melissa had been one of the five students chosen to go on the three-week field trip to the deserts of Utah, she hadn't really wanted to go, but hadn't felt she could refuse the honor. But when Donny had taken a seat next to her in the van on the way down, she'd started counting herself lucky. Until that moment, she'd been ready to quit the rigorous program, go back to the little cottage her parents paid for, and keep creating the cute, but uninspired, little pieces of pottery she sold on Etsy. Now, with Donny, she never wanted the course to end.

Donny powered the Jeep up the last ten impossible feet of the slope. It was wildly exciting. Melissa couldn't ever remember feeling this way, taking these kinds of chances. It was only momentum that kept them from toppling over; then they were at the summit. Despite herself, Melissa let out a big sigh of relief. Donny looked over and laughed.

"Look," he said, pointing at the two hills on the horizon. "Pyramids."

She could totally see it. Rising above the flatness of the rest of the terrain, the hills looked like giant structures built by an ancient people no one had yet discovered. That was the way Donny saw it. On her own, Melissa would have seen a couple of unremarkable hills.

"Let's walk there, little Owl," he said.

Melissa wore large, round glasses. From anyone else, she might have been insulted by the nickname, but Donny said it with such affection that she'd come to like it even when the other students picked it up. Petite and dark, Melissa knew she was beautiful, but she'd always hidden her body beneath baggy clothes and gone without makeup because she didn't want the attention.

Now, for once, she really wanted a guy to notice her.

There was just enough room at the top of the hill to turn the Jeep around and point it back down the road. Melissa's faith in Donny's judgment was once again rewarded. He always seemed to be pushing the edge, but when you followed him there, you realized there was another edge beyond it.

She reached into the backseat and grabbed her backpack. The hills were several miles away, at least. In the desert, distances could be misleading. She wished they could drive there, but it looked like Donny had indeed reached the place "where the roads end."

There was a deer trail that led down the other side of the hill, and they started descending. They hadn't gone more than ten feet when they heard a noise behind them, the almost metallic clattering of shale sliding down toward them. Donny grabbed Melissa as she stood there with her mouth open and pulled her out of the way. The rockslide barely missed her.

Donny held onto her, and she wanted to melt into him, but he looked distracted—and there was something in his eyes she'd never seen before: doubt.

"Maybe this isn't such a good idea," he said. "Come on, let's drive back down and see if there isn't an easier way to get there."

She nodded, disappointed when he let go of her, but appreciative when he put his strong hands on her back and helped push her to the top of the hill.

The Jeep was surrounded by pigs. Hairy, ugly pigs.

Donny stopped, and his hand went to the knife at his belt. "Shoo," he said to the animals.

It should have been an enchanting moment, a brush with the local wildlife, but there was something odd in the way the pigs were arrayed: not at random, but almost in ranks. And there was a pig in front that was simply enormous, half again as big as the others.

It grunted, and several of the smaller pigs trotted forward, coming directly at Donny. He pulled out his knife and waved it at them, but they keep coming. Then they were swirling around his legs. Donny stabbed downward, but didn't seem to hit anything. Then he let out a cry of pain. Melissa wanted to run to him but was frozen in fear.

Suddenly, Donny was on his knees. He'd dropped the knife and was clutching his ankles. Blood was welling over the tops of his shoes, soaking the yellowish slate.

The big pig trotted forward, his head now at the same height as Donny's. They seemed to be staring into each other's eyes.

Then Melissa heard Donny say defiantly, "Fuck you, pig."

The animal slammed into Donny's midsection, and he slumped over. Something wet and pinkish-white and visceral sloshed onto the ground in front of him, and he let out a ghastly rattle as if he was already dead and his last breath was slowly being released.

He toppled over and fell into two parts. The lower part of

his body went backward, the top of his torso went forward, and the insides splashed wetly between them. Melissa saw a look of horror in his unseeing eyes. And then she was screaming and screaming. She must have started running, because she slammed into the rear door of the Jeep. Luckily, they hadn't bothered to lock it, and she scrambled inside.

She hid in the foot space behind the passenger's seat, breathing hard, that last image of Donny frozen before her eyes. She began to cry and moan, her mind blank, feeling only terror. How long she quivered there she didn't know but, eventually, she heard the animals outside, scratching at the Jeep as if trying to get in. She heard them underneath the vehicle, too, but she slowly realized they couldn't get to her. That should have been reassuring but their purposeful efforts to get inside the closed Jeep were frightening. That wasn't something animals would normally try to do.

Then the Jeep lurched. Melissa cried out, suddenly remembering the steep sides of the hill and how close she was to the edge.

The vehicle started sliding, and then her world turned upside down. Melissa was slammed against the Jeep's roof, then back onto the seat, then against the roof again. She heard bones breaking and saw red blood splash against the shattered windows. She tumbled faster and faster, and the bottom half of her body was flung through one of the broken windows. The rocks of the hillside squashed her between them and the Jeep, severing her in two, and then only the top half of her was tumbling inside the Jeep, still conscious, until the vehicle landed on the flats below.

Melissa wasn't breathing any more, but she still had a few moments of consciousness—just long enough to see the huge pig staring at her from outside the wreckage, its intelligent eyes watching her die.

She felt Donny's spirit nearby and wished she still had the breath to say, "Fuck you, pig."

# Chapter Two

Lyle Pederson's Last Will and Testament, besides making Barry and Jenny Hunter wealthy beyond their wildest imaginings, contained a clause that Barry had memorized, he'd read it so many times.

*"I want you to find out if we got them all. Every single Tusker. Because if we didn't, it won't be long before there are new litters of new Tuskers. So I'm asking you to track down any survivors and kill them. Don't hesitate. Don't try to capture them.*

*"Just kill them."*

Well, that was the question, wasn't it? Barry ran the last few minutes of the conflict over and over again in his mind. Had they gotten them all?

He was certain the Tuskers' leader, Razorback, was dead, finished off by his own progeny as he lay mortally wounded. Barry had later retraced his steps and found the bodies of Reagan and Thatcher, riddled with bullets. Himmler had died with Lyle's arrow buried deep in his body. Barry himself had killed Stripe.

At least three Tuskers, including Vader, had followed Barry into the box canyon and been blown to smithereens. When Barry had returned to his home, he'd found another, unnamed Tusker in the bedroom, killed by Barbara Weiss before they had overwhelmed her.

That was nine Tuskers in all: a large litter, but not unusually so.

The question was…had they missed any?

The days after the battle were so filled with activity that Barry

didn't have time to think about it much. He was released from
the hospital after his second day there. He had a concussion,
and the doctor told him to stay home for a few days. Other than
a headache and the Tusker slash on the sole of his foot, which
was healing, he was fine.

Their home was completely destroyed, but even if he and
Jenny could have restored it, he suspected that the odor of pig
shit would always linger, at least in their imaginations.

They lived in Lyle's (now theirs) high-tech barn for those
first few weeks. The old man's house might have been more
comfortable, but Lyle's presence was too strong in there.
They spent long days in the lawyer's office. The will having
been changed only a day before Lyle died made the whole
thing somewhat suspicious. Even worse, the witness to the
notarization of the will was missing. (The probate court ignored
the strange, non-legal requests in the will, though the judge
raised his eyebrows at them.)

But in the end, the notary public, Bart Hoskins, vouched for
the legitimacy of the document, and since Lyle had no known
relatives to dispute the will, Barry and Jenny inherited over
a thousand acres of prime Morrow Valley land and a bank
balance that had a single large prime number followed by more
zeros than they could count in one glance. All from a man they
had barely known only a week before.

*"Don't hesitate. Don't try to capture them.*

*"Just kill them."*

Lyle had bought so many supplies in preparation for
Hamageddon (which was what Jenny was calling it) that the
Hunters didn't need to go shopping for months. They stayed
inside, licking their wounds, which were mostly psychic, not
physical. As the days passed, the whole incident seemed more
and more unbelievable, preposterous even.

But they needed merely go up the spiral staircase to Lyle's
crow's nest to find confirmation that it was all true, it had all
happened. Even without using the telescope, they could see the
blackened walls of the box canyon where the Tuskers had met
their end.

*"I want you to find out if we got them all. Every single Tusker."*

They took a couple of lawn chairs up there and sat for hours, inspecting their huge new domain.

"I watched you every step of the way," Jenny said one afternoon. "Do you know how many times they almost caught you?"

"I was trying not to look back," Barry admitted. "I knew they were close."

"When you disappeared over the edge of the canyon, I wasn't sure what to do. I saw Lyle get tossed into the air and fall. He stopped moving. But what…what if he was still alive?"

Barry shook his head. "He wasn't. Believe me."

"I suppose I knew that," Jenny said. "And I knew that Lyle wouldn't have wanted me to abandon my post."

"How many Tuskers did you see?" Barry asked. "At the end?"

"Through the telescope, it was hard for me to tell which were Tuskers and which were just normal javelinas," Jenny said. "I mean, Razorback was hard to miss. He was twice as big as any of the others."

"But you saw the three that tried to get me when I was climbing?"

"I couldn't believe it. They seemed to be climbing the rope after you!"

"They were propping each other up, babe. They weren't actually climbing the rope."

She shook her head wonderingly. "Still…"

Barry looked over at her and laughed. Jenny was tall and willowy, her hair still blonde though she was a couple of years older than him. In comparison, he was gray and balding, and out of shape—though less out of shape after all the recent activity.

"Pigs don't fly," he said. "That's the last thing I said to the one I kicked in the tusks."

Jenny joined his laughter but it was a little forced.

Barry tried to keep his voice casual. "But you only saw those three, right?"

She nodded. "Are you still thinking about that?"

"It was the only thing Lyle asked for in return for all these riches," Barry said. "...to make sure the Tuskers are all dead. Seems like the least I can do. Think about it some."

"But you're thinking in circles, honey. We've had no sign that there are any still alive."

Still, something was nagging at Barry. He just couldn't put his finger on it.

*I want you to find out if we got them all. Every single Tusker. Because if we didn't, it won't be long before there are new litters of new Tuskers.*

Barry jolted awake in the middle of the night.

*Genghis.* The Tusker with the Fu Manchu-looking tufts of hair on his face. Had he been one of the last three Tuskers to follow Barry into the canyon? For the life of him, he couldn't remember. But he had a sinking feeling that Genghis hadn't been there.

He looked over at his sleeping wife and thought about waking her up and asking her, but he doubted she could have seen that level of detail in the telescope.

Genghis was still out there, Barry realized.

*"I'm asking you to track down any survivors and kill them.*
*"Don't hesitate."*

Barry lay awake the rest of the night.

# Chapter Three

In 1781, Spanish explorers (who were barely aware that a new country, what would eventually be called the United States of America, was being born on the other side of the continent, a country that would eventually overwhelm their descendants) became lost between Santa Fe and the new mission in Los Angeles.

They camped in a steep canyon between two hills, where a small spring emerged and whose water saved their lives. They stayed there for a week, recuperating, before moving on to the west.

Later, they could not say exactly where they had stopped. But one of the explorers, a young and naïve priest named Father Herrera, had spied some shiny pebbles in the waters of the spring and put them in his pocket. Upon arriving at his new home in Los Angeles, he pulled them out, tossed them onto a table in the great hall, and left them lying there.

A day later, he found one of the soldiers assigned to the mission leaning over the table. When Father Herrera entered the hall, the man turned to him with round eyes. "Where did you get these?" he asked, holding up one of the gleaming stones.

The good father told him about the spring between the hills.

"Show me," the soldier demanded, bringing out a map.

Father Herrera looked over the map. He had no idea where he was, much less where he had been. But the man was insistent, so he took a wild guess and pointed at a spot.

The soldier reached over and marked it with an X.

So went the story, and when Martin Bleecker bought the map,

along with the story, more than 230 years later, his friends laughed at him. But Martin had spent every dime he had on the map, so he took it to an expert on old books and manuscripts, who confirmed that the paper and ink were old enough to be genuine.

Martin sold his car and every other possession that was worth anything, went to a gold mining store in Albuquerque, and bought the cheapest usable equipment he could find.

"This stuff will work," the clerk commented dubiously, "but it won't hold up for long."

"If I don't find something quick, it won't matter," Martin said.

In the back of his mind, he suspected that he'd be better off taking his meager life's savings and betting it all on black at a roulette wheel in Vegas, but this seemed like a more industrious way to self-destruct.

*This will take longer and hurt more,* he thought. *Just as I deserve.*

And if God wanted to save him and show him the gold, then that would be a sign that he deserved to live after all.

Truth was, he'd always planned to disappear this way, to give people a legitimate reason why he'd go into the wilderness and vanish. That way, the life insurance company would have to pay up. Martin had been a lousy father, but he could do that much, at least. He was either going to strike it rich or disappear.

He had just enough money left on his last viable credit card to rent a pickup from a local car rental place. The only vehicle he could afford that had a high enough clearance to handle the back roads was an ancient Ford F-250.

As he bumped along roads that didn't look like anyone had driven down them in years, Martin told himself it didn't matter if the truck died now. He was so near the trailhead.

He parked, gathered up his backpack and shotgun. He'd loaded himself up with food, but only enough water to get to his destination. If the spring wasn't there, he was doomed.

He took his cellphone out. It was running at 25 percent power, but he still had service for the time being. That wouldn't last, not out here. He called the car rental joint. He was just as glad when he got the message service.

"Hi, this is Martin Bleecker. Please take note. I've left your rental at a turnoff eighty miles down Fire Road 206. The keys are under the front seat." He hung up, stashed the phone along with the keys, and locked the doors behind him. *No second thoughts. No retreat. Burn all bridges.*

As he walked away, he felt bad about abandoning the truck. He'd always been a very responsible person. Always living by the rules. It had driven Julie crazy. Hell, it had probably driven Julie away. He was, "No fun," she had informed him. Even Clarice had acted bored with him the last time he'd visited, and that had broken his heart. His only child had always been so happy to see him before. But she was turning into a teenager and seemed embarrassed by him now.

Martin realized he'd walked far enough that he couldn't see where he'd parked the pickup anymore. It wasn't really that far, what with the undulations of the high desert and all, but he was already sweaty and grimy and tired. By his calculations, he still had at least twenty miles to go, probably more than he could travel on foot in one day.

He took out the map and compass and oriented himself. The guy at the outdoor store had given Martin a crash course on orienteering, so he had a general idea of how to do it, though as he looked around on this cloudy day, he realized he might actually be heading in the exact opposite direction from the one he wanted to go in.

The whole plan was half-baked and desperate. But then, Martin never would have undertaken the expedition if he hadn't been that far gone.

One night a few weeks back, he'd been lying awake, suffering buyer's remorse for purchasing the map, when an idea had occurred to him. He'd thought at one point in his life of being a geologist. The math had proven too hard, but he'd learned enough to know that gold mining fields ran along certain topographical features.

He got up and Googled the known gold deposits in the Utah area, and drew a line following them north to south. Then he drew a line showing the east-to-west route of the lost Spanish expedition. Where the two lines met, he was certain he'd find the lost gold.

He showed his best friend, Rollie, his discovery.

"Assuming your map is real," Rollie said in his commonsense way, "the Spanish were lost and only guessing at the route they took. Then, assuming the story is real, it could just as easily have been a few gold placer deposits that didn't amount to much. And finally, the point where these lines intersect is, in reality, probably a hundred square miles. You could spend the rest of your life searching an area that big."

"But I only have to find two hills close together, with a spring between them," Martin objected.

Rollie looked at him with pity. "Have you ever been out there? Even in the high desert, there are a lot of hills. How big are the two you're looking for? How close together?" He shook his head. "You couldn't have a more vague location, description, and story than what you've got."

Martin knew Rollie was right. Rollie was almost always right. His wild and crazy friend from high school had married his college sweetheart, Melanie, had a brood of kids, worked his way to an engineering degree, worked for the city of Phoenix for thirty years, and retired early with a passel of grandkids to occupy his time.

For some reason, he was a faithful friend to Martin. He always had been. When Martin had been fighting depression during his senior year in high school, Rollie had come to roust him out of bed every morning and haul his ass to school. When Martin couldn't find a job after college, Rollie had let him camp in his garage for a couple of months. (Melanie had rolled her eyes, but she loved her husband enough to put up with it.)

To everyone's surprise, Martin had made a career out of his geekiness, selling pop culture stuff in a downtown store. Even more surprisingly, he'd married a young woman later in life and had a kid.

What wasn't so surprising, perhaps, was that Julie had then taken him for everything he was worth.

When Julie kicked Martin out of their house, Rollie came through again, loaning him enough money to rent an apartment.

In fact, it was fear of becoming dependent on his friend that was responsible, as much as anything else, for this harebrained scheme.

Martin checked his compass again, then walked due east, away from his past, into a desperate gamble of a future. Deer trails led in the general direction he wanted to go, and he followed them as much as possible. Inevitably, he needed to course correct by tacking overland. He waded through the sagebrush, certain that deer ticks were covering him from head to toe. He would need to do a thorough search of his body that night.

*No mirror*, he thought. *I should keep a record of how many things I forgot.*

Dust streaked his legs, and the bottom of his shirt was covered with burrs from a particularly nasty plant. He kept going until he found a single rock jutting out of the sand, and he rested there and took his first drink of water.

Despite Rollie's comment, there were no hills in sight.

*What do you know, Rollie was wrong about something.*

The landscape wasn't exactly flat, though. It was filled with gullies and small rock outcroppings and the occasional slope that could be called a hill. It was exhausting, unpredictable footing, with every step slightly higher or lower than the last, and it was making Martin's muscles tense up with every stride.

He saw tracks along the deer trails that he was sure weren't from deer, but he didn't know what to make of them at first. Then he saw a pack of javelinas in the distance.

He trudged on for a while, not thinking about it much, then stopped short. There, standing in the middle of the trail, was a large javelina. It was watching him...no, *examining* him, as if taking his measure.

Martin slid off his backpack. He'd strapped his shotgun to it, and he now removed it. The javelina disappeared before he was through arming himself. Martin carried the shotgun as he continued down the trail.

The backpack stopped chafing as much, and Martin was glad for that. But now the shotgun was getting heavy.

The gun was almost an antique, hefty and ornate. The guy

at the gun shop had offered him more money for the shotgun than Martin had gotten for his car, but there, Martin had drawn the line. It was the one possession of his father's that he still owned. He had the gun guy clean it and fix it up, and bought a box of shells.

He hadn't really expected to run into any danger out here. (In the back of his mind, he'd wondered if he would resort to the shotgun in the end, if his slow demise was too painful.) But now he remembered the news stories from a couple of weeks before about rabid javelinas in the neighboring state of Arizona, in the town of Saguaro, and he was suddenly glad he had the weapon.

Martin didn't see any more wild pigs for the rest of the day. As dusk fell over the landscape, it became harder to gauge the hollows and depressions he was walking through. The wind picked up late in the afternoon and gusts blew sand in his face.

*A handkerchief and sunglasses*, he thought. *Add those to the list of things I forgot.*

He found a small hollow surrounded by rocks and decided it was as good a place to camp for the night as any. He soon had a sagebrush fire going, had laid out his sleeping bag, and was roasting a hot dog.

He should have been comfortable, but he had the sense that he was being watched. When the fire died down and he crawled into his sleeping bag, he laid the shotgun across his knees.

Martin spent the night staring into the dark, listening.

When he awoke, the feeling that someone was watching him was stronger than ever. There was just enough dawn light to see the raven staring down at him from the log where he'd sat the night before. From where he was lying, it looked huge.

It cawed once, loudly.

"Caw, yourself," Martin mimicked, and it came out as a surprisingly accurate echo. It seemed to surprise the bird, too, for it rose with a huge flap of its black wings, a whoosh of compressed sound, kicking dust into the coals of the fire. Martin's gaze followed the raven, then stopped as the shadow passed by the single juniper tree at the edge of the clearing.

It took a few seconds for him to realize that what he was seeing wasn't the foliage of the tree, but black birds that covered every inch of its branches. As one, they took flight, crying out in a cacophony of caws that sounded like a warning and a threat, a swirling cloud that loomed over him for a moment, then fluttered away to the east.

Then there was just the desert silence. Martin almost wondered if it had been a dream. He fell into a troubled sleep.

# Chapter Four

Months passed with no sign of any Tuskers.

The county's javelina population started to recover, and Barry kept a close eye on them, but they were your everyday kind of peccaries—annoying, but hardly dangerous.

Barry was rich beyond imagining, but he couldn't enjoy it. He'd been a lot less stressed when he'd been an ordinary middle-class retired guy with half his net worth eaten up by debt.

"I'm not doing enough," he said to Jenny, a familiar lament. "There has to be a way to find them. Something I'm not thinking of…"

"You're doing the best you can," she answered. "Something will pop up. And if nothing pops up, that's even better, right?"

Barry wasn't so sure. He was now convinced that the Tusker called Genghis had escaped. If there were no hints of his location, well, that only meant the pig was smart enough to hide his whereabouts, which was alarming in itself.

"Jenny," Barry said. She looked up at him from her book and sighed. She knew when he was going to go off on one of his rants. "Pigs can have two litters a year, up to sixteen pigs per litter. They become sexually mature in six months. So…I can't do that math, but if you start exponentially adding up the numbers, we could be in real trouble."

"Yeah, well," she said, "if it was that easy, all pig farmers would be rich. And the Tuskers are in the wild, foraging for food, prey to predators and disease."

"I suspect the Tuskers are the predators, not the prey," Barry said darkly.

"Still, it's probably not as bad as you're imagining,"

Jenny insisted. "Besides, maybe it was only that one litter of Razorback's. Maybe they're infertile, or can't pass on their intelligence."

"Maybe," But it didn't matter whether that scenario was likely or not. Lyle Pederson had asked him and Jenny to make sure the Tuskers were extinct, so he had to keep looking until he could determine once and for all whether there were any survivors.

Barry hadn't gotten the idea of autopsying the Tuskers until a full week after the fight. Unfortunately, by the time he retraced his steps back to the gully where he'd shot the two Tuskers, Reagan and Thatcher, there was nothing left but a few scattered bones and dried skin.

Meanwhile, rather than trying to repair their own modest house, which was riddled with holes the Tuskers had created trying to get in and covered with blood and pig shit, the Hunters had decided to tear it down. One afternoon, staring absently at the construction—or rather, destruction—Barry was struck by an idea.

He called the contractor and asked him what had happened to the pig corpses.

"I buried them in a trench out back," the man said.

"Meet me there in an hour," Barry commanded. "Show me."

They dug up the bodies, and in among the smaller javelinas was the large carcass of the Tusker that Barbara Weiss had killed. For once, Barry was lucky. The temperatures had dropped below freezing for several weeks after the burial, and the body was in relatively good shape.

Barry flew in an outside expert, Dr. John Harvey, a forensic pathologist, who swallowed his umbrage at being called on to do an autopsy on a pig when he was offered twice his usual fee. Barry put him up in the best inn in town, a B&B down by the state park.

"Treat this as a real autopsy," Barry said. "I want you to examine every part of the body. But pay particular attention to the brain."

"With what you're paying me," Dr. Harvey said, "I'll pretend it is Napoleon's body. I'll get back to you in a couple of days when all the lab results are in."

Instead, the doctor called twelve hours later, at 11:30 at night, as Barry was going to bed.

"Is this a joke?" the pathologist demanded.

"Is what a joke?"

"Did you put a human brain into that animal?"

Barry felt a chill race down his spine. He knew that the Tuskers were something new...but he'd been hoping for a different explanation. "Tell me what you found."

"Well, the brain in this animal is bigger than that of most humans, and that is extraordinary. But even more importantly, the outer cortex is extensively developed with sulci and gyri."

"Which means?"

"Widespread grooves and bumps, which in humans is thought to indicate intelligence. The intracranial folds in the brain are far larger than most people's. If this were a human, I'd say he was probably the most brilliant person alive. So I ask you again, what kind of hoax is this? I'm assuming that you've concocted this thing, assembled it somehow."

"I assure you, Dr. Harvey, I haven't tampered with that pig." There was a long silence on the other end of the phone, and Barry began to wonder if they'd been disconnected. "Doctor?"

"I'm going to have to publish these findings," the doctor said excitedly. "This is miraculous!"

"You will not, Dr. Harvey. Not if you want to be paid."

The man laughed. "Screw your money. This will make me famous."

Barry felt a cold resolve come over him, like nothing he'd ever felt before. He'd always gotten along with other people, usually by going along with them, or at most, trying to bring them around to his point of view if there was a difference of opinion. But he now had the money to get his way.

"This is what will happen, Dr. Harvey," he said coldly. "I will spend my considerable resources to discredit you, which shouldn't be too hard, since you have to admit your results are pretty unbelievable. You will not be allowed to take the body of the Tusker, thus, you will have no evidence beyond pictures and tissue samples. You will be sued and taken to court, and if you have done anything inappropriate in your life, I will find it. Anything at all: failing to pay your taxes; cheating on your college exams; cheating on your wife; shoplifting as a child."

Barry sensed that his threats were having an effect, so he changed back to his customary, more moderate tone. "But if you do as I say, I will pay you quadruple your regular fee. Plus, you have my assurance that when the time comes for this to become public, you will be the first to publish."

"Tusker?" the doctor said, after another long silence.

"What?"

"You said Tusker…is this a new species? Is that what we've found?"

"*We* haven't found anything, Doctor. *You* are a hired gun—a highly paid hired gun."

"How can I help?" Dr. Harvey asked, his voice now subdued. "I'd like to get in on this. What can I do?"

Barry hadn't expected this offer, but the answer immediately came to him. "My math is a little weak, Dr. Harvey. I'd like you to figure out how many of these creatures could be conceived over…let's say two years, with each litter being ten pigs and an average fertility age of six months."

"I can't do it, not without knowing how many breeding females there were at the start…but I can tell you this: it could be in the thousands, or tens of thousands. Exponentially, the number could be enormous."

Now it was Barry's turn to be quiet.

The doctor spoke into the silence. "Mr. Hunter. I noticed that the cadaver had a bullet hole in its chest. Are these…Tuskers… dangerous? Shouldn't we let the authorities know about this?"

With all his heart, Barry wanted to dump the problem on the authorities. But Lyle had been convinced that the government would try to study the Tuskers, to keep them in captivity, and that the Tuskers would outsmart them and escape. Lyle had advocated killing every Tusker. 'Species survival is at stake,' was the way he had put it. 'The human species.'

As squeamish as the idea of genocide made Barry (and Jenny was utterly opposed to it), he'd committed to wiping out the species if possible. But truth was, if he did find the Tuskers, he wasn't sure he could go through with it. He'd been living off Lyle's bequest, but he'd decided he would give it all back if he found he couldn't follow Lyle's instructions.

But with what Dr. Harvey had just told him about Tusker intelligence, he was starting to wonder if Lyle hadn't been right.

The Tuskers they'd fought had been the first generation, without any culture or history behind them, without any technology.

And those Tuskers had almost won.

# Chapter Five

Flaco Morales looked in the mirror the first morning after returning from vacation and grimaced.

He'd spent his working life protecting himself from the sun, wearing long-sleeved shirts, boots, jeans, and a Stetson hat. Then, after a week lying on the beaches of Hawaii under the very same sun, he was as tan as he'd ever been. He always had a dark V of skin at the top of his chest, and a bleached tuft of chest hair, but now the rest of his body almost matched it.

He'd made a good decision, getting out of town. Just as he'd figured, there'd been something off about the javelinas. The way they'd been acting had scared him so much that he'd pulled his daughter away from teaching her third-grade class (a sudden case of the flu was the explanation she'd given the school), along with his five-year-old grandson, Felix. It was time for a vacation anyway, and that annoying real estate agent who'd been bugging Flaco to sell some of his Morrow Valley farmland so he could put up another subdivision had conveniently handed Flaco a nice check for a pretty useless acre of land (no doubt believing that once Flaco got a taste of the money, he'd break down and sell more).

The real estate agent, Peter, hadn't survived the holocaust that had overtaken the town.

The authorities were blaming rabies, but Flaco could tell they were hiding something. The death toll hadn't been as bad as it looked at first. Most people had the sense to stay indoors, though when the water was cut off, and the electricity, some were forced to venture outdoors.

Somehow, Lyle Pederson had lured all the javelinas into a

box canyon and blown them to smithereens—along with himself.

*It was all very strange and unnatural, and Flaco figured there was more to the story…much more.*

"Papa!" Alicia's voice sounded like it had when she was a little girl and it was her birthday.

Flaco hurried into the living room, where Alicia was talking excitedly into the phone. "I'll come and get you," she was saying.

"No," said her husband, Enrique Flannigan, on speakerphone. "I'm already here, so I'm going to rent a car and drive home. No sense both of us making the trip."

Flaco shook his head. Enrique was always commonsensical, always matter of fact. Truth was, Alicia would have loved the anticipation of driving to Phoenix, and would have been thrilled to drive back with her husband, to have him all to herself.

"By the way…did I mention that I'm a staff sergeant now?" Enrique asked casually, but with a hint of pride in his voice.

"Oh, honey! I'm so proud of you!" Alicia exclaimed.

"No big deal. Stay in the Army long enough and you're bound to get promoted eventually."

*Not true*, thought Flaco, who'd never risen above the rank of corporal when he'd served in Vietnam. He spoke up. "Are you done? Or are those bastards sending you back again?"

"Papa, now is not the time," Alicia protested.

Both men ignored her. "I don't think they'll send me back," Enrique answered. "A deployment in Iraq and two deployments in Afghanistan is probably more than enough. Though…well, you never know."

Flaco was as patriotic as the next guy, but he'd been outraged when they'd sent his son-in-law on his second tour, much less his third. "We'll be here waiting, son," Flaco said.

"Can I talk to Felix?"

"Felix is at a sleepover with Parker," Alicia said. "Remember, that's his best friend?"

"Sure, Parker Stevens. Though I think I always called him Steven Parker."

Alicia laughed. "Hurry home, sweetie." She paused. "But drive carefully."

This time Enrique laughed. "Don't worry. I haven't spent five years dodging IEDs only to die in a car accident."

Flaco gave his daughter a hug after they hung up. She was shaking from excitement, her eyes shining, an animation to her movements that he'd missed seeing.

Alicia took after her mother in looks. Flaco was short and dark; his wife had been tall and red-haired. Maria had covered up her freckles with makeup, but Alicia let hers show.

Despite his half-Mexican heritage, Enrique was tall and blond, like most of the Flannigan side of his family. He'd been the Big Man on Campus in high school, and Alicia the quiet, studious one. He'd been All-State, and she'd been salutatorian. Flaco wasn't sure they'd even known each other back then. But when they'd gone to the local community college, they were immediately drawn to each other. Alicia had been the popular one in college while Enrique had struggled to find his way.

When he'd failed geology class, he'd enlisted in the Army, but not before he and Alicia eloped and got married without anyone knowing. Flaco was still a little bummed about that, though he sometimes winced when he thought about how his family and the Flannigan family had interacted at first.

Once everyone realized how happy the couple was, though, their gatherings had gone more smoothly. And when Felix was born, that had sealed the deal for the extended family. (Despite his tall, blond dad and tall, red-haired mom, Felix looked like Flaco, his "Granda," small and dark.) Now the Flannigans and the Morales's got along great.

Flaco wondered if Enrique was aware he was returning to what had been, not so long ago, a war zone itself. Should he even bring it up? *No*, Flaco thought. *No sense worrying him.*

It was only a couple of hours' drive, and Enrique would be home by 1:00 p.m. As he watched Alicia bustle around the house, Flaco decided he'd take Felix and absent himself from the house for a few hours later that afternoon, after the homecoming, so the young couple could be alone.

He'd heard that Lyle Pederson had willed his land and what was apparently a great Silicon Valley fortune to Barry and Jenny Hunter. No one knew why. No one was even aware they'd been friends, though they'd lived near each other.

Flaco tried to recall what the snowbird couple looked like. He couldn't visualize Barry, but he was pretty sure that Jenny was the statuesque, good-looking blonde woman he saw downtown sometimes. The one that reminded him of his own Maria. Newcomers came and went in the valley, came and went. They thought the rural life was what they wanted, and then got lonely or bored. Or worse, they bought a farm and tried working it for a few years, then got tired of waking up at five in the morning to milk the cows and feed the chickens and horses.

But the Hunters, if he had the right couple in mind, had seemed like the kind who would stick to it, who had known what they were in for when they moved down here. He vaguely recalled liking them.

He decided it was time to reintroduce himself.

"Wait here," Flaco told Felix, and got out of the battered pickup.

There was no one home at the old Pederson homestead. No one answered his knock on the door or his calls of "Hello?" Flaco looked in a couple of the windows, and it appeared that the rooms had been stripped of furniture.

The original one-room cabin had been added onto by each generation so that the house now sprawled over a fifth of an acre. This land had once belonged to the Morales family. In fact, they had owned most of the valley for hundreds of years, before the U.S. had even been formed. During the Mexican-American War, one of the patriarchs had been smart enough to choose the Americans over the Mexicans, so they'd managed to keep their land.

The Pedersons had been the first gringo family to move into the valley from the East, joining the Morales clan, and the two founding families had always cooperated, down to the current generation. Lyle and Flaco had both agreed that there was enough development in the valley and that neither of them would sell any more land. It had driven the real estate boosters crazy. Flaco wondered if the new owners of this land, the Hunters, understood the unwritten agreement.

Not only wasn't anyone home, the entire place looked abandoned. Yet something about the setup looked familiar, somehow...and then it came to him. He recognized it from his time in Vietnam. It was disguised, but once he saw it, unmistakable. There was a defensive perimeter around the farm, constructed from fences and hay bales and farm equipment—subtle, but obvious to someone with an experienced eye. The ground was churned up, as if a hundred pairs of feet had marched over it, and here and there was a thicker layer of dirt that Flaco somehow understood was covering up blood.

Flaco heard a buzzing sound from the barn, a hundred yards away. The barn itself was, upon closer examination, a fortress, reinforced along the sides, with portholes that could be used to shoot out of.

He found Barry Hunter cutting two-by-fours on a couple of rickety sawhorses. The barn's walls had been reinforced up to about five feet, and it looked like Hunter was raising the reinforcements even higher. Flaco stood off to one side until Barry was done sawing, knowing better than to surprise a man who was using an electric saw. Then he moved slowly into Barry's line of sight.

Even so, the man jumped a foot, letting out a surprised cry.

Flaco held his hand out in a peacemaking gesture. "Sorry," he said.

"No, no," Barry said, looking chagrined. "I'm a little jumpy after everything that's happened."

"That's what I'm here about," Flaco said. "I was out of town and have only heard conflicting rumors since getting back."

"You're Mr. Morales, right?"

"That's me. Lyle Pederson and I were friends, but he never mentioned you."

Barry nodded matter of factly. "That's because, until right before he died, Lyle and I hadn't said more than five words to each other."

Flaco raised his eyebrows, waiting for the explanation.

"Lyle left a note about you," Barry said. "He said you guys had an agreement not to sell any more land. I want you to know I'll abide by that agreement. But I should probably tell you everything that happened. I warn you though, you probably won't believe me."

"You might be surprised," Flaco said. "I didn't go on vacation when I did by coincidence."

Barry examined him, then nodded again. "Why don't you come inside and meet Jenny? I'll do my best to tell you what happened, though it'll sound like a tall tale."

"Sounds good," Flaco said. "Do you mind me fetching my grandson? He's in my pickup."

"Go get him. We'll be waiting inside the barn. We're living there now. Feels safer than the house."

Flaco resisted asking more questions, figuring Barry Hunter would spill it all once they were inside. Nobody in the valley talked about what had happened, as if none of them thought anyone would believe them. He walked over to the pickup, thinking over what he'd seen so far.

The Barry Hunter he remembered meeting had been a chubby, genial snowbird who seemed intent on doing as little as possible. This new man had angles, and a weathered look, and the kind of economy of movement that a man of action developed. Flaco remembered the same look in the eyes of veterans in Vietnam when he first arrived there, and the same look had been in his eyes when he'd been shipped home.

And this new Barry Hunter had a gun holstered on his hip, with the flap already open for quick access.

Felix was waiting patiently in his car seat, his eyes just showing over bottom of the window. Flaco unstrapped him, but let him get himself down and out of truck. The impulse to lift him and carry him everywhere was nearly irresistible, but Flaco thought it important that the child make his own way. *Even the child restraints in vehicles seemed unnecessary*, Flaco thought; somehow, his generation had survived without them.

Felix marched determinedly behind Flaco, who took a step or two and paused, pretending to search his pockets or some other piece of business until the child caught up, and then doing it again.

"Look, Granda," Felix said. "A piggy!"

Flaco whipped around, surveying the horizon, and saw the

animal come around the side of the house and freeze at the sight of the humans.

It was the biggest javelina Flaco had ever seen, the size of a wild boar, the kind he'd seen in Texas on his way to Vietnam. But its hair and much of its skin had been burned off, and the rest was red and blistered or black and flaking, with yellow pus oozing from the cracks. The skin around its mouth was burned away, and all that was visible were brown teeth and two impossibly long tusks. One eye was dead, milky white, but the other was yellow and enraged.

It charged.

Flaco reached for his knife, but he'd left it at home. He and Felix were halfway between the pickup and the barn, and there was no cover in sight. He scooped up Felix, who felt as light as a feather, unceremoniously threw the child over his shoulder, and ran for the open door of the barn.

The animal surged forward, grunting, huffing as it ran as hard as it could to catch him, running at an angle that Flaco saw would cut off his route to safety.

He stopped, reached down, and picked up a small rock. He threw it at the pig, hitting it in the face, but it merely grunted, lowered its head, and kept coming.

Flaco wanted to reach down and engage the creature, but that would bring Felix into its range, so he stood at his full height and prepared to try to dodge its attack instead. He would stay upright as long as possible, even if its tusks tore into him, anything to keep Felix out of the monster's reach.

He saw the puffs of dirt rising from the ground before he heard the gunshots. They were like tracers, and he watched the puffs march forward until they reached the pig and threw the animal to one side. It squealed and landed on its back, then righted itself just as another wave of bullets cut it nearly in half.

The hate in the animal's eyes still burned. In its last moments, it dug its tusks into the hard ground, and dragged a four-inch-deep groove there. Flaco shuddered at the thought of what those tusks could have done to soft human flesh.

The pig quit moving. The light went out of its eyes.

Flaco turned to see a slender, middle-aged blonde woman

lowering an AK-47 that had obviously been modified to fully automatic. She smiled at them and waved them over.

Felix didn't object when Flaco swung him around into his arms and carried him the rest of the way. The child was quiet. Flaco wondered how much he'd seen or understood.

The woman was older than she'd looked at a distance, and Flaco realized that it was Mrs. Hunter. He'd admired her from afar for a long time, but had never actually met her.

"I'm Jenny," she said in confirmation, putting out her hand. "I'm sorry that I'm such a bad shot. I've only fired this thing a couple of times. After this, that is going to change. I can't afford to miss like that."

"Well, we used to say in Vietnam, it isn't how good a shot you are, it's how many bullets you have," Flaco said, shaking her hand. He grinned. "Or was it the other way around?"

He followed her into the barn. It looked like the Hunters had hauled the beds, couches, tables, and chairs over from the house and laid them out in the semblance of a living room and bedroom in the open expanse of the huge barn.

They all sat down at a small, round table, and Barry brought over a six-pack of Coke. Felix gladly took one and guzzled it down. After a moment of hesitation, Flaco also took one, cracked it open, and took a sip. "Now," he said, after a big sigh. "You want to tell me what that...*thing*...was?"

Barry and Jenny Hunter looked at each other, and some understanding must have passed between them.

Jenny spoke softly. "That, Mr. Morales, was a Tusker."

# Chapter Six

After a sleepless night of starting awake at every sound, Martin almost turned around toward home. He was willing to die, but he wasn't sure how uncomfortable he wanted to be while doing it. After a breakfast of hash browns and bacon, he was ready to move on.

Bacon. He'd always known he'd have to hunt for his food after the first few days, and seeing the javelinas was confirmation that that was possible.

He reached the spot on the map where he thought the hills should be, but there was nothing but a barren landscape. There was one high hill to the east, so he headed that way. When he came around the side of the hill, he saw the wreckage of a Jeep lying on its side. With his heart in his throat, he approached, afraid of what he'd find. He'd never seen anyone dead before, and he didn't want to start now.

The Jeep was empty. There were some dried bloodstains, but no bodies. Barry was relieved. No doubt the wreck had been discovered and the victim or victims removed. Martin started to walk away and tripped over something white lying on the trail.

It was an arm, with part of the hand still attached: three bony fingers and a patch of skin.

He backed away, nearly tripping on a rock, but when he looked more closely, he saw that it wasn't a rock but a skull, with some black hair still clinging to it. A beetle, disturbed in the middle of its meal, crawled out of one of the eye sockets. It was a small skull—a woman's or a child's. Which could mean there were other bodies.

Martin turned away, walked shakily out of sight of the bones, and sat down.

The vehicle had come crashing down from the top of the hill, he could see that from the extent of the damage. The person whose body he'd found had probably been thrown from the vehicle and crushed. It was tragic, but it was none of his business.

But what of the relatives? Didn't they have a right to know what had happened to their loved one (or loved ones)? How long before someone else ventured this far into the middle of nowhere and stumbled across the wreckage? Maybe never.

He saw movement from the corner of his eye and stood, fumbling for his shotgun. The feeling of danger that the ravens had imparted, whether in a dream or in reality, came back in full force.

It was coyote, which stopped in the middle of the trail and stared at him insolently.

"Get out of here!" Martin shouted, and the coyote started but stayed put. A few moments later, three more coyotes came out from behind the hill and also stopped and stared at him.

Martin sat very still. The coyotes radiated menace, though he'd never heard of a coyote attacking a full-grown man. In fact, he'd only ever seen the hindquarters of a coyote, running away, weaving among the junipers. These coyotes were all large and male, and Martin was pretty sure that was unusual. Coyotes were solitary creatures, weren't they?

He raised the shotgun, and as if that was a signal, the four coyotes turned and trotted away, still maintaining that aura of insolence and menace.

*Strange*, Martin thought. *There's something very odd about this place.*

He put the shotgun back and sat down in the dirt again. He put his head in his hands. He thought about the wrecked Jeep and the bones he'd found.

*I will have to go back*, Martin thought, then laughed. He shook his head at the irony. He'd been willing to let his own family suffer, not knowing what had happened to him, but he didn't want some unknown family to suffer that way?

Absurd as it seemed, the answer was apparently yes.

Yet...the dead were dead. So it wasn't like it was an emergency. At the least, he decided, he should continue his search until he ran out of food. Then he'd return to the truck and hope there was still enough juice in the phone to call for help.

He continued around the base of the hill, then stopped in his tracks.

There, rising from the desert floor like two pert breasts, were two hills with a narrow divide between them, as if someone had cut between them with a knife. Martin couldn't believe it. He'd expected to search for days, weeks, most likely forever for the twin hills, which on the map were called Tetas de Bruja— Witch's Tits.

It was too easy. How was it possible they hadn't been found before by one of the previous owners of the map? Martin had a sinking feeling. Perhaps they *had* been found. Perhaps the gold had been removed, or worse, had never been there in the first place.

But then he realized that he had access to technology unavailable to previous generations of treasure hunters: a readily accessible topological map, accurate GPS coordinates, and geological surveys. He'd been able to find them in a few short days of research on the Internet, whereas in the old days, it would have taken months of research and travel to find the information, if it could be found at all.

Maybe, just maybe, he was the first.

Martin reached the hills in what seemed only minutes, but turned out to be well over an hour. The canyon between the hills was so narrow that he couldn't see inside it until he was directly in front of it. By then, the sun was falling below the horizon.

He hadn't brought a flashlight. *Add it to the list.*

Morning would come soon enough. He set up camp right outside the entrance to the canyon and lit a big fire. There were some downed junipers nearby, and he felt like celebrating. Tomorrow he'd know whether he was rich or whether he needed to return to the truck to inform the authorities about the accident. Either way, it would be an eventful day.

Amid all the excitement, Martin completely forgot about the javelinas. As he lay down to sleep and the crackling of the fire died down, it seemed to him that he could hear the burbling of water emanating from the canyon. When he really tried to listen, the sound faded. But each time he gave up and started dozing off, he heard it again. The map had clearly indicated water.

So the night passed, without much sleep...but unlike the previous night, when he couldn't sleep because of fear, this night, he couldn't sleep because of hope. His eyes popped open every few minutes, and once again he had the feeling that he was being watched.

When Martin awoke, the morning sun shone directly into the canyon, as if it had been aligned just for him. Not wanting to lose the bright light, he hurriedly dressed and headed in, leaving most of his things behind. The gully couldn't have been more than a few hundred yards long. It was at a slight incline, and despite what it looked like from a distance, it didn't go all the way through the hills.

The sound of water echoed through the narrow canyon. It was a splashing sound, not a flowing sound, and there was no evidence of water in the lower, sandy parts of the passage. The "spring" turned out to be a small waterfall that emerged exactly halfway between the two hills, about eight feet up a steep cliff. The smooth canyon walls on either side looked sheared off.

The water flowed down to a catch basin, not much bigger than a bathtub, but didn't overflow the stone enclosure. *It must filter through the sand below*, Martin thought, *and return to the water table*. The sunlight was shining directly onto the pool, and Martin realized that if he had come at any other time of year, he might not have seen the glittering nuggets in the sand below the shimmering surface. He fell to his knees, closed his eyes, and thanked the god he didn't believe in.

He sidled up to the side of the pool on his knees. He reached down into the water to grab one of the shining chunks of metal that appeared to be only inches below the surface. He reached in up to his forearm, then his elbow, then all the way up to his shoulder, and still he couldn't reach the rock.

Without thinking, Martin plunged into the pool, head first. The water was freezing cold, bracing after the already-warm morning sun. He nearly took a breath of water in shock, but kept reaching down. His hands brushed the sand, and then his fingers touched something solid.

Martin rose, gasping, laughing, and holding the rock up to the light. It was a dark piece of the surrounding granite.

"Shit!" he said.

Before he could second-guess himself, he plunged in again, this time with his eyes open, aiming for one of the glittering stones. He grabbed it and immediately felt the weight difference from the first rock. He surfaced and held it up out of the pool. It was about an inch wide, half an inch thick, and half an inch long. It was without a doubt gold, judging from the weight alone.

Martin's whoops and shouts echoed down the canyon, so it sounded like a party of men had made the greatest discovery in history. In stirring up the sand, he'd uncovered many more nuggets. He plunged all the way into the pool, knowing the sun would dry him out in minutes, and grabbed a handful of the nuggets, which seemed to want to drag him down as he tried to lift them.

He tossed the gold out of the pool and went down for more, and more…until, exhausted and giddy, he climbed out, sat next the pile of nuggets by the cliff, and ran his fingers through them.

As he was sitting there, his eyes followed the path of the little waterfall to the hole it emerged from, and he saw a glint, right on the edge of the hole, and realized that the gold was coming from inside the cliff.

*Who owns this land? How do I go about claiming mineral rights?*

It was something he should have thought of before, but of course, he hadn't really believed he would succeed. Perhaps the best thing to do was haul as much of the surface ore away as he could and come back for more when he needed it.

It would be a shame to tear down this beautiful oasis.

Nevertheless, Martin knew he wouldn't be able to resist. He'd buy the rights or the land, whatever it took, with the money from these nuggets. And he'd tear into that cliff until he had every bit of gold, until he was so rich that his daughter would never want for anything ever again.

He heard a slight sound behind him, like someone clearing his throat. When he saw the javelina, the sound was transformed into a grunt. It was the huge pig Martin had seen on the trail, and this time, he was accompanied by an entire pack of his smaller brethren. They jostled for space, filling the narrow canyon as far as Martin could see.

He reflexively reached over his shoulder, as if he was still carrying his pack with the shotgun attached to it, but he'd left it beside his sleeping bag. He hadn't even brought his knife.

Not that he would have had much of a chance against this brute. The monster's tusks were half a foot long and curling, unlike the smaller, straight tusks of the other javelinas.

The leader of the javelinas came closer, and Martin backed away until he was pressed against the rocks of the cliff. His hands landed on the nuggets, and for a wild second, he thought of throwing them at the huge javelina.

The pig seemed to be reading his mind. Martin saw a look of what appeared to be amusement in his eyes, and—as if that wasn't weird enough—the animal shook his head from side to side in a very human way.

*I wouldn't do that if I were you*, the gesture said.

The pig grunted loudly, with a complex series of sounds. Two javelinas turned and made their way out of the canyon, pushing through the crowd of other pigs. The leader turned and regarded Martin again.

When Martin tried to stand up, the hair bristled on the tops of the creature's jaws. He grunted a warning, and Martin flopped back down again. The pig had a long mustache hanging down the sides of his snout, like an ancient Chinese scholar's. His eyes, full of intelligence, only added to the image. *Genghis*, Martin thought. He didn't know where the name had come from, but he was certain it was the right one.

*They're waiting for something*, Martin realized. As he

watched Genghis, he saw that several of the pigs near him were extraordinarily fat.

*Those sows are pregnant,* he intuited, *with Genghis's progeny.*

There was a disturbance at the back of the crowd, lots of grunting and squealing, as the two messengers returned. One of them was carrying something in his mouth, and it wasn't until he dropped it in front of Genghis that Martin could make out what it was: a blackened branch from the campfire.

*Why did he...?* Martin began to ask himself.

Genghis picked up the unburned end of branch in his teeth, walked to the cliff face, and started brushing the burned end over the smooth stone.

Martin couldn't make sense of the action. Then his heart seemed to skip a beat, and he gasped.

*Stay.* The word was clearly written.

Genghis kept writing.

*or*

Martin realized he had been holding his breath and took a big gulp of air, on the verge of passing out.

*die.*

Martin stared, his mouth open, and looked into the deep-set eyes of Genghis and knew it wasn't a trick. It wasn't an accident.

*Stay or die.*

Martin finally managed to nod, when he realized the javelina was waiting for an answer. "I...I don't understand," he muttered. "How...?"

He was already dumbfounded at the thought of a pig writing words. But when the pig spoke, he nearly collapsed.

"Teach," Genghis said in guttural but clear English. "Stay and teach."

# Chapter Seven

Barry had found, somewhat to his surprise, that he didn't care about money—or at least about the luxuries money could buy. But he had also found that cash did have its uses when trying to get one's way.

The Saguaro city commissioners sought him out, and he told them no, he wasn't going to be selling any more land, and neither was Flaco Morales, and they'd have to be satisfied with living in a farming community with a small enclave of snowbird retirees.

He also made sure the library, parks, and other civic-oriented town services and amenities were well funded. He made low-interest microloans to small businesses struggling on Main Street and to small farmers. He bought parcels of land from the few landowners who had parcels to sell. Eventually, enough money was floating around the little town of Saguaro that almost everyone was satisfied.

And he started to expand his fortress.

From the outside, it still looked like a large barn, but it had odd outbuildings scattered about. There were covered walkways between the buildings. Fences were everywhere, sometimes noticeable, sometimes not.

That was strange enough. But what was inside, what no one saw, was even stranger. Tunnels had been built in every direction, and storage areas and dormitories, enough for everyone who lived in the valley. Though the residents didn't know it, there were enough beds, food, and water for everyone. When the Tuskers returned, everyone would have a sanctuary to go to.

"How do you even know there are more Tuskers?" Flaco asked on one of his frequent visits. They had become close friends. Flaco and Jenny especially seemed to get along. "We haven't heard a peep out of them."

"They're out there," Barry said. "I can feel it."

"Well, it's your money," Flaco shrugged. "At least you're putting people to work and spreading it around."

Barry added up the bills every month, and to his surprise, more money was still coming in than was going out. Lyle Pederson had invented some sort of component that was used in every cellphone, computer, and tablet device in the world. Each piece was only worth a few cents, but there were billions of them, more all the time.

Meanwhile, the Hunters' new friend Flaco was struggling. His farm wasn't doing well no matter how hard he worked. The weather had changed just enough that the crops he'd always grown weren't thriving, and the new crops he was trying were hit and miss. His money problems would have been instantly solved if he sold some of his land, but because of his agreement with Lyle and now with Barry, he was prohibited from doing so.

It wasn't a legal prohibition, only his word—which turned out to be more binding than any piece of paper could ever be.

So Barry bought up the acres of land that were of no real use to Flaco. The farmer had refused at first, until Barry had plunked down his laptop and shown Flaco the spinning numbers in his bank account, dollars rolling in every second of every minute of every hour of every day...

"Hell, Flaco. It's not like I earned it," he'd said.

"Very well," Flaco had replied. "For the sake of my Alicia, and Enrique, and Felix, I will accept your money."

One night, they were sitting around drinking some very expensive wine (Barry's one luxury) after Flaco had been given a tour of the new facilities.

"It's all very impressive, Barry. But don't you think it would be better to tell the authorities?"

"I promised Lyle Pederson."

"You did not," Jenny objected. She'd been arguing the same point as Flaco from the beginning. Barry wondered if she had put him up to it. "It was a deathbed request, but you weren't given a chance to refuse."

"I took the money," Barry said stubbornly.

"So give it back," Flaco said. Money meant even less to the farmer than it did to Barry.

"Would you so easily break your word, Flaco?" Barry thought that would be a winning argument, because he knew how much pride Flaco took in his word of honor.

"I would if it was for the greater good," Flaco said, surprising him. "If breaking my word would save lives, I wouldn't hesitate."

"You didn't see them, Flaco. I believe those Tuskers were evil. They wanted to kill us all."

"But can you be so certain that they are *all* evil? What you're planning on doing is killing off an entire species. Would humanity pass your test any better, if we were all judged by the worst of us? Why do we deserve to live more than these Tuskers? There is evil in us as well."

"Fair enough," Barry said. "But what if it's them or us?"

"Barry, they are *pigs*," Flaco said, his big, dark eyes wide. "You can't really believe it would come to that."

Barry fell silent. Truth was, the more time passed, the more unbelievable those events seemed. Had they really nearly been killed off by bands of wild pigs? How could these animals possibly be a threat to humanity at large? Surely the authorities could control the situation.

"Besides," Flaco continued, "what makes you think they'll return here? And what makes us special? Why should we be protected by Mr. Pederson's money while everyone outside of this valley is on their own?"

"I'm sure they'll come back," Barry said, not really sure at all. "This is where they were born."

Flaco drained the rest of his glass in preparation for leaving. "I have one last question. Suppose you and Lyle are right. What if the Tuskers really are a danger to humanity? What if the menace is too big for you? Shouldn't we make sure that the governments, the police, and the military are also prepared?"

Barry didn't say anything. He had all the same doubts. Many a time, he'd come close to picking up the phone and calling the cops, dumping it all on them. He had his doubts they would do anything, or would do enough, but certainly they had resources that even a billionaire couldn't summon.

But...there had been no word of the Tuskers, and if it was all over, why get everyone all riled up over nothing? Besides, was there any chance they would believe him? Even with the evidence he could present?

So he struggled with the decision.

There was one other thing he didn't mention. If the problem was already solved, if the Tuskers were gone, then the money was his, forever, because he'd kept his word. No harm, no foul.

He was a little disgusted with himself at the thought.

Apparently the money meant more to him than he wanted to believe.

But he had to admit, he was getting used to it.

# Chapter Eight

Martin heard a loud, impatient grunt behind him and turned from the rock wall he was using as a chalkboard. He was diagramming the Battle of Salamis, where the Greek states had turned back the Persian Empire. The grunt had come from one of the newer students. This particular pig always seemed to speak up when the subject was warfare.

The Tusker held up a small slate board. "Why do humans fight each other?" the slate read. "Why do they not cooperate?"

*They never ask the easy ones*, Martin thought. *It's as if they don't have any time to waste on simple questions.*

Martin sighed and tried to come up with an answer that would satisfy the insatiable curiosity of the Tuskers. "Truth is, I don't know," he said. "Oh, humans fight for resources, for power, for land, for pride, for religion…but none of that is completely right. I think we fight because we fight, because it's in our nature."

One of the Tuskers grunted something, and the other pigs huffed in what Martin had learned was their laughter. He had picked up a tiny bit of their language, and realized the Tusker had said, *"Monkeys."*

As if Martin had given him a real answer, the Tusker began scratching furiously at the small slate on the floor.

The classroom was carved into a sandstone cave, which might have seemed primitive if it hadn't been lit by an electric light. In Martin's mind, the room suddenly appeared as another human—who didn't know about Tuskers—might see it. Martin almost laughed out loud at the image. Over thirty pigs of all shapes and sizes were sitting on their haunches in front of him, with those strange devices on their front hooves that allowed them to grasp objects. They were paying attention to his every word, as if he knew what he was talking about.

*How the hell did I end up here?*

He remembered when they'd first led him into the pig settlement, dazed, not quite believing that he wasn't hallucinating, perhaps wandering the desert on the verge of death.

"The humans call us Tuskers," their leader, Genghis, said to him when he first arrived at the settlement. It was bustling with pigs of all sizes, with coyotes at the fringes who seemed to be taking orders, and flying overhead were squadrons of ravens, who appeared to be delivering messages. "Teach us what you know."

Martin had found himself bowing to the huge creature. The Tusker radiated power and intelligence, and something more— Martin caught him glaring, and realized the pig hated him, hated all humans.

All of the Tuskers had understood what Martin was saying from the first, almost as if they could read his mind, though very few of them could actually speak. They scratched out their questions, and he answered in English.

He settled in and realized, one day, that months had probably passed. He couldn't be sure how long it had been, but it seemed like he'd been there for a lifetime. He was starting to understand some of the Tuskers' complex arrays of grunts and squeals and snorts. He was beginning to be able to read their expressions. They were so human-like that sometimes Martin forgot he was different from them, and then, suddenly, he would realize he was teaching arithmetic to a classroom of Tuskers, and he'd become almost dizzy from the surrealness of it.

It was frightening how intelligent the Tuskers were. They were smart beyond belief. He usually only had to teach them something once and they remembered it. He'd thought at first that he'd be teaching at kindergarten level, or perhaps grade-school level—rudimentary writing, spelling, and arithmetic— but after each new litter was introduced to basic concepts, they quickly advanced.

In the beginning, Martin used crude blackened sticks and wrote on the stone cliff side. Eventually, the Tuskers began rotating classes into a schoolroom they carved into the hillside just for him. And they refined the process of making charcoal writing tools.

Genghis denied Martin's every request that he be allowed to leave, to get textbooks with which to teach, even though Martin promised not to betray them. Instead, books began showing up in the classroom cave, with tooth marks on the covers as if the javelinas had bitten down hard on the precious tomes. Martin welcomed the books, for he was hungry for diversion himself, and because he was running out of things to teach. Other human objects began showing up, too, and Martin realized that the pigs were foraging for things to bring back for their pet human.

So Martin taught them the essentials: the alphabet, then reading, then basic arithmetic. He talked about history and sociology and every other subject he could think of, and they listened to him. He was somewhat surprised by how much he knew—and it was all revelatory to the pigs. He was also surprised by the huge gaps in his knowledge base.

They soaked it all up, every bit of it. The pigs grew up so fast that what Martin might consider to be a first-grade class would advance to the level of a sixth-grade class in mere weeks. Sometimes he'd start telling a new class of pigs something and one of them would grunt at him to stop, indicating that they already knew it—which meant that information was being passed along without him, that once he taught a group of Tuskers something, they took that knowledge and taught it to others on their own.

Obviously, he was only the starting point. They were getting their higher education from the books they were bringing back from the scavenger hunts in the surrounding territory.

A few days previously, he'd walked into one of the rooms next to his classroom and found that it was filled with Tuskers with books spread out in front of them, all of them reading. Another pig stood before the wall at the front of the room, writing with a piece of charcoal in its mechanical hands.

*I've landed in* Animal Farm, Martin thought, restraining a panicked giggle. *All pigs are equal, but some pigs are more equal than others.*

There was a loud, impatient grunt, and he was brought back to the present.

His aggressive questioner was holding up his slate as if challenging Martin to a duel. "If it is their nature to fight," it read, "why do humans not change their nature?"

*Why indeed?* Martin looked out over his classroom, and instead of laughing, he suddenly felt sad. The full class time wasn't up, but he just didn't feel like teaching anymore that day. He set down the charcoal. "Before you start asking more questions I can't answer, I think that is enough for today."

The questioning pig looked up, glaring, as if he was going to object. A smaller female Tusker beside him grunted something softly, as if in warning. The bigger Tusker looked away. When he turned back again, his expression was blank. The pig picked up his slate in his teeth without comment and left the classroom.

But Martin had seen that momentary flash of hate. That hate was always just under the surface with some of them. It always shocked him when it saw it.

Soon he was left alone, wiping the day's lessons from the wall with a soft, frilly cloth the Tuskers had provided him. He looked down at the fabric and realized it had come from some kind of blouse. He sniffed it and smelled a faint perfume. A sudden longing to talk to another human washed over him.

He sat on the floor, put his head in his hands, and fought off tears. He'd always thought of himself as a recluse, always trying to get away from people. He never would have thought it was possible, but he was lonely.

The Tuskers treated him with deference, but most of them weren't friendly, and he was becoming more and more isolated. At first he'd been fascinated by it all. It had never occurred to him to leave. But sometimes, the strangeness of his situation would overcome him and an unexpected nostalgia would wash over him. Sometimes he wished he could have a normal, humdrum conversation with another person, even if it was only about the weather or the price of peas.

Besides, what would happen when the Tuskers sucked him dry of everything he knew?

He shook his head at the thought. There was a suspicion in

the back of his mind that they didn't really need him, that he was a pet, or worse, a caged zoo animal. Nothing more than an example.

He rubbed his face one last time and got up from the floor. He picked his books up off the desk. The classroom was on the ground floor of the western hill. He had been given a small room to sleep in on the other side.

He walked out, blinking, into the desert sunlight, surprised as always by the brightness.

The javelinas had burrowed into both of the Witch's Tits. They had even carved out rooms and corridors. Martin didn't think burrowing was normal behavior for pigs, but he wasn't sure. Then he laughed at the thought. As if any of this was normal.

It was difficult to get an accurate gauge of the number of animals, but one thing was for sure: it wasn't in the dozens, as it had been when Martin first arrived, nor even in the hundreds. Martin thought it might be in the thousands.

The burrowing wasn't so much for shelter, he suspected, as to hide their numbers.

The encampment was made up mostly of normal javelinas, who were called the Folk. The highly intelligent pigs called themselves the Kin. Together, they were called the Kinfolk. Martin quickly learned to discern which javelinas were Folk and which were Kin. It wasn't only that the mutant pigs were bigger; there was also a presence about them, a sense of self-knowledge and personality.

Troops of javelinas marched out every morning, each troop led by one of the Kin. They were being forced to range far and wide to find food and supplies for their ever-increasing numbers, along with the occasional human item for Martin. The majority of the Folk spent the daytime either inside the caves or out in the high desert. Only at night were their real numbers revealed to the outside world.

But that wasn't even the most remarkable thing. Martin had noticed large groups of coyotes near the fringes of the camp. At first, he had been amazed that they were running in such big packs, for coyotes were usually solitary or found in small family units, as far as he knew. Then, one day, it had struck him: the coyotes were under the influence of the Kin. Sometimes one of the Kin would walk right up to a pack of coyotes and seem to communicate with them. The coyotes would tilt their sharp little snouts as if listening, and then run off together as if commanded.

There were also large flocks of ravens and crows hanging around, and again, Martin thought that there was a connection there. Ravens would land near one of the Kin, and then fly off as if on a mission.

*Somehow,* Martin thought, *the Kin can communicate with and control these other animals.* They were probably using the same nonverbal, perhaps telepathic, method they used to control the lesser Folk.

Maybe telepathy explained how they always seemed to understand what he was saying to them. *They* can *read minds,* he thought, not for the first time. And not for the first time, he rejected the thought.

*Why do you reject it?* said a voice in the back of his mind. *Why would that be any stranger than any of the rest of this?*

Martin passed by the rock wall where he'd found the vein of gold. He hadn't glanced that way in a long time and was shocked at the change. The water from the fall was being diverted. The gold had been tossed to one side of the canyon as though useless. Cisterns had been built all along one side of the hillside—though they were so well disguised that the wells weren't visible from more than a few feet away.

He entered the residential corridors under the hill, which were empty, as usual during the day. Electric lights ran along the top of the hallway. He reached his room without seeing anyone. They'd made a crude wooden door for him, which fit imperfectly into the sandstone opening but which gave him at least the illusion of privacy. The gaps around the door let in enough light from the hallway for him to be able to see.

It was a roughly carved room, with few comforts. He'd pulled pictures out of books and put them on the walls to add a little color, but other than that, the only human touches were some blankets on the floor and an old, beat-up school desk that they'd scrounged from somewhere and that was piled with books and papers.

Martin lay down on his moldering pile of blankets.

*Why am I still here? Why am I teaching these alien creatures? Am I being a traitor to my own kind?*

For the first time, he started contemplating escape. The world needed to know about this miracle. These animals were more intelligent than most humans, that much was clear.

He closed his eyes and tried to think of way to get away, and then wondered if he *should* get away. Still trying to think of the right thing to do, he fell asleep.

It was dark when he opened his eyes again.

Someone was in his room.

"Excuse us, sir," came a rough voice, the guttural sound of a pig speaking English.

Martin had been given a small electric lamp, which he sometimes used for reading at night. He turned it on to find the door to his room open. He recognized the small pig in the doorway as one of his *favorites*.

It had occurred to Martin one day that a few of the pigs kept returning to his class, even though he had already taught them the subjects they were sitting in on. He began to recognize them, and to assign them names. The pig who'd awoken him had an unusual shade of red to his patchy hair, and Martin had secretly begun calling him Erik the Red. Behind Erik was another one of his favorites, a small pink female he'd begun to think of as Petunia.

*Not very professional, having favorites,* Martin thought. But then, he wasn't a professional teacher.

Martin suspected their attention wasn't completely altruistic, that they had been assigned to watch over him. Yet he often found himself talking directly to them over the heads of the rest of the class. They watched him with eyes that were curious and somehow comforting. It took a while, but Martin finally began to think that they actually liked him and wanted to be around him.

*How strange,* he thought, *that they should even care.*

His own kind had cared not at all when he'd lost his business, his family, his reasons for living.

"May we come in?" Erik the Red asked.

"What is it?" Martin was alarmed. He'd never been visited in his own room before, and he was afraid that he'd gotten his friends in trouble by treating them differently.

Erik started to ask a question, but the words came out jumbled. Among Martin's favorites, Erik had always had the most trouble speaking English. While the Kin wrote or spoke in a kind of Pidgin English, it didn't mean they were stupid. They were simply being more efficient in their communications, like the younger generations of humans who were learning to shorten their messages by texting.

Frustrated, Erik snatched a piece of charcoal and started writing on the stone floor. "Leave others behind?" he wrote.

"Others?" Martin asked, confused. He'd told them all about human society. They knew that over the horizon were endless numbers of men and women, cities and towns, and machines and electricity and...

Petunia stepped forward and nuzzled Erik. "He means close..." she hesitated, struggling to find the right words. "Close...Kin?"

"Oh, you mean my friends and family?" Martin asked.

The pig gave a small nod.

"I am alone," Martin said, without thinking. He immediately realized how true that was, and it was the most desolate moment of his existence. Perhaps his daughter might miss him for a few months and wonder about him as she got older, but to most of the world, it didn't matter that he had left the scene.

Erik bent down and wrote again. "We be friends," he wrote.

Martin stared at words for a few moments as the message sank in.

Unexpectedly, his eyes filled with tears. It was the last thing he'd expected, but when he looked into their eyes, he saw that they meant it.

Erik grunted something, then leaned down and underlined the word *friends*.

Martin said, "Thank you, Erik." He turned to the female and bowed slightly to her. "You too, Petunia. I do believe I could use some friends."

# Chapter Nine

One of Barry's biggest expenses was the battery of lawyers he'd hired. (Well, maybe "hired" wasn't the right word. He had them so tied up in legal obligations that he *owned* them. This power thing could be addicting, he was discovering.)

As Barry expected, the forensic pathologist, John Harvey, couldn't stay silent and tried to publish a paper on his findings. When he couldn't find a legitimate journal to accept his paper, he approached the mass media with his story.

Barry's lawyers had prepared a barrage of negative stories about the good doctor, but it didn't prove necessary. The scorn and derision that Harvey suffered was more than enough to shut him down. Barry began to think of the leak as a good thing, for it inoculated the press for the next revelation, whenever and however that happened.

The doctor was destitute when Barry approached him again and put him on the payroll, after he signed papers that had Barry owning everything but his soul.

The small amount of publicity did have one other benefit.

Not long after the Harvey debacle, Barry got word that a visitor was in town, sniffing around, asking odd questions. When the man inevitably showed up at his gate, Barry let him in.

"Dr. Oliver Patterson," the stranger said by way of introduction.

"What can I do for you, Doctor? We're all very healthy here."

"What...? No, I'm a professor of biology, at the University of Oregon. I believe that something happened in this valley, and you were at the center of it, Mr. Hunter."

"Come on in, Dr. Patterson," Barry said, leading him toward the barn. He stuck out his hand. "Barry," he said.

"Ollie," the professor said, shaking it.

The visitor was looking around curiously, with sharp eyes. When he was seated at the dining room table (which sat in the middle of the cavernous barn), he asked, "Are you expecting a war? Or perhaps a plague?"

"Why would you ask such a thing, Ollie?"

The professor smirked but didn't answer. Barry suddenly decided he didn't like the man. But now that he was here, there was no sense not feeling him out, finding out what he knew. "What do you want, Ollie?"

"I want real answers. Everyone in town is very closed-mouthed...as if they are afraid of you, or have been bought off. But this rabies outbreak you had here seems very strange—first, in that it affected only javelinas. That's not how rabies works. Rabies can infect any kind of mammal. Second, there is the fact that there are no bodies, no evidence. Third, I found a strange report from a reputable pathologist theorizing that a new species had been found here."

"Reputable?" Barry asked skeptically.

Patterson flushed. "He was reputable until he spouted off without evidence. Still, as strange as his account sounds, it is, so far, the only explanation that makes sense. You see, Barry, I've been waiting my whole life to see a species make such an evolutionary leap. It was the subject that got me a cum laude from Harvard. It was my doctoral thesis at Brown."

"And that was, Doctor?"

"That the environmental stresses brought about by mankind would quicken evolutionary change in other species. But I was beginning to wonder if I was wrong. I mean, my research is sound, but there should have been evidence by now. I was certain it would happen in my lifetime. And now...I believe it has."

"I have no idea what you're talking about." Barry just couldn't bring himself to keep calling the man "Ollie."

"I think you do, Mr. Hunter."

*Buy him off or shut him down?* Barry wondered. Seeing the

mulish look on the professor's face, he suspected that trying to buy him off would only backfire. Barry sensed this man wouldn't retreat, wouldn't give up when the going got rough, like Dr. Harvey had. This man would only get more adamant, more fanatical the more pressure he was put under.

"Out of curiosity, Dr. Patterson, what would you do if there *was* a new species?"

"Why, study it, of course. But I would also prepare for the worst, make sure that I had a defense against it." He looked pointedly around at the reinforced walls of the barn, his eyes lingering on the closed gun locker and then traveling to the stacks of supplies in the back of the barn. "I'd need to have some research money, however, to do the job properly."

*Oh ho! So that's what this is about,* Barry thought. The way it had been presented made him reject the idea. "I wish you luck with that," he said, standing up. "I'm a careful man, Dr. Patterson. Any number of disasters can happen, and if they do, I'll be prepared. Seems like a prudent thing to do when you have the money."

"Seems reasonable to me," the professor said, also rising. "Especially if you know as much about disease as I do." He put out his hand, and Barry shook it after only a moment of hesitation.

They stopped at the gate. "I want you to know, Barry, I intend to keep looking, keep asking questions," Dr. Patterson said. "Nothing you can say or do will stop me."

"I hope you find what you're looking for," Barry said. "Far be it for me to stop scientific progress."

The professor turned to walk away. "I'm heading up to southern Utah," he said, looking over his shoulder. "There's been an unusual population explosion of javelinas there. I asked for some satellite data. And here's the really strange thing: there appear to be artificial structures right in the middle of the javelinas' territory. Structures that shouldn't be there."

He got into his yellow van, which had the big green O of the University of Oregon on the side, and waved nonchalantly as he drove away.

# Chapter Ten

Martin's little band of favorite Tusker students quickly grew. He taught regular classes during the day, and at night he would hold seminars in his room with what he considered his graduate students.

There was the small female, Petunia, and of course there was Erik the Red. Also coming to most meetings was Goliath, whom Martin suspected had been assigned to be his watcher. There was another young female, Marilyn, who had blonde hair that was thick about her head, and the mild-mannered Gandhi, who was always trying to moderate arguments. There was King, who was a Tusker who also professed pacifist beliefs. King was a huge Tusker, almost as big as Goliath, but whereas Goliath seemed strong and powerful, King's bulk was mostly fat. He waddled when he walked.

These six were the nucleus of Martin's *followers*, though others regularly accompanied them. Some attended for a while and then disappeared. Others stayed around longer, or came intermittently.

In reality, there wasn't much Martin could teach them. By now, the Tuskers were teaching each other far faster than he could. The Tuskers had managed to bring in generators and to set up rooms with computers. They were off limits to Martin, but he sometimes walked by and saw his former students staring at the screens. He realized that they were going far beyond what he was teaching.

His classroom teaching also changed. No longer did he monologue off the top of his head about any piece of information that came to him. Now his students were asking him frighteningly intelligent questions, most of which he didn't know the answers to.

"What is electricity? How is it generated?"

"At what temperature is steel smelted? How do you create such temperatures?"

"Why do humans use up all resources?"

"What is God?"

One day, as Martin stood flabbergasted in front of the classroom, unable to articulate a coherent answer to one of these questions, he realized his students had moved beyond him, that he had taught them everything he knew. He was still useful with the very young ones, though even there, he suspected that the pigs were able to teach much faster and more effectively than him and that they were simply humoring him.

Once again, Martin had the suspicion that to most of his students, *he* was the lesson. *Look!* they seemed to be saying in those moments he caught them off guard. *This is a human. Observe him, learn his behavior.*

Martin began to look forward to the end of the school day, when he could be with his teacher's pets again. All this socialization had the effect of lessening Martin's desire to escape. At one point, he realized he felt more accepted, more a part of a group, than he'd ever felt in his life, and he didn't know whether to laugh or cry at the thought.

One night, Erik the Red was having particular trouble pronouncing an English word. Finally, he wrote the word "friend" on a slate. He grunted, underlined the word on the slate, and grunted the same sound.

Martin suddenly understood what the pig was trying to do. "That is the Tusker word for friend?"

Erik nodded.

Martin tried to replicate the sound, and the pigs looked at each other and made strange huffing sounds that Martin realized was laughter.

"Sorry," Petunia said demurely. "But you described a bodily function."

Martin tried again and again until Erik grunted as if to say, *That is acceptable.*

So began Martin's turn to learn. His students-turned-teachers were patient with him, for it took him much longer to absorb things than it did them. He realized, when he had a vocabulary of about a hundred words, that the grunting he'd heard around him all day, every day, had been constant conversation, a complex language that he hadn't had a clue existed.

*They treat me like a dumb child,* he realized. It hurt his pride a little, but he couldn't deny the truth of it. These animals were far above him in intelligence.

Finally, he couldn't resist asking his favorites what he'd been wondering for some time. "Why do you come to me?" he asked. "I have nothing left to teach you."

"Yes, you do," Marilyn said. "You teach us what it means to be human."

"Why do you want to know that?" Martin asked, curious.

Petunia spoke up. "Humans are complex creatures. We have much to learn from them."

*But why?* Martin thought but didn't ask. "You have your own culture here in Pigstown," he insisted. "You don't need me."

"Pigstown?" Goliath rumbled.

Martin flushed. To himself, he'd begun to think of the settlement by the admittedly inelegant name. "I'm very sorry," he said. "Perhaps you have a better name for it?"

"Don't be sorry," Goliath said. "We just call it Home." It was reassuring that this response came from the huge Tusker, who said so little and who was always so imposing and solemn.

"You aren't...insulted?" he asked Erik, his closest Tusker friend.

Erik shook his head. "Why should we be? In your eyes, that is what we are. We are pigs."

"You're sure you don't mind?"

The Tusker gave a nearly human-looking shrug. "It is a good reminder to us of our origins, and how hard it will be to convince humans to think of us differently."

"So you don't mind that I give you human names?"

"It is helpful," Petunia informed him. She was by far the best at English, though she was perhaps overly precise. "Naming does not come naturally to us. We have never had names for ourselves. We recognize each other by sight and smell. But it is useful to have a name when the individual is not near, so we have each decided to have identifiers. Your names are more… evocative than ours, which tend to be descriptive names like Longsnout or Curved Tusk. I *like* Petunia."

After that seminar, a young pig who was attending for the first time, named Leonardo because of his interest in art, came up to Martin.

"Martin," he said shyly. "You asked why we study humans. May I show you something?"

"Sure," Martin said.

Leonardo was already trotting off, obviously expecting Martin to follow. They left his room and went into the hallway and turned right, heading farther into the hillside. He'd been down there a few times, but most of the rooms farther in had doors, and it had seemed obvious to him that he wasn't welcome there.

At the very end of the hallway, there was a large door, which Leonardo pushed open. There was natural light on the other side, so different from the electric light in the hallway. Martin stepped in, almost blinded by the sun pouring through a skylight in the huge room. As his eyes adjusted, he began to see grooves carved into the sandstone walls. They were fluid and serpentine and beguiling. His eyes couldn't help but follow them as they wound in and out of the crevices of the cave, and it took a few moments for him to see that there was representational art there, figures of Tuskers and humans and other animals.

It was breathtakingly beautiful, and Martin felt a frisson run down his spine and tears come to his eyes. "You did this?" he breathed.

"Me, and others." Leonardo inclined his head, a humble gesture. "But none of this would exist if you had not exposed us to human art. *You* are responsible for this."

"You…you would have done it on your own."

Leonardo was shaking his head. "No. This…art…does not come naturally to us. We had to be taught to appreciate it, to understand it."

"Looks like you learned well," Martin said.

When he went back to his room that night, Martin was once again convinced that he was doing a good thing by staying and teaching these Tuskers. Surely beings who could create such beauty were worth saving, worth lifting up. He no longer had any doubt that these creatures had souls.

After that, Martin starting naming every Tusker he met with the first name that popped into his head. It wasn't long before the Tuskers began to name themselves, most often following the example of their leader, Genghis, and naming themselves after famous humans.

"All very highfalutin," Martin said one day, after being introduced to a Cleopatra. "But most humans don't make the history books. They have names like Fred and Muriel."

"Then again, we are the first generations of the Kin," Goliath responded calmly. "We will be long remembered by those who follow us. There will be time for Freds and Muriels later."

Science wasn't Martin's strongest subject, so he was intrigued whenever one of his students took the little snippets of scientific information he gave them—general background, really—and ran with it. One day, while he was talking about the development of electric lights and the duel between Edison and Tesla, one of his newest and youngest students suddenly perked up and began asking questions. The next time the Tusker came to class, he asked questions about Tesla that Martin couldn't answer.

"I don't know," Martin finally exclaimed in frustration. "Why don't you research it yourself? Meanwhile, I think I've found the name for you. From now on, I'm going to call you Tesla."

The young Tusker seemed pleased by the name.

At first, Tesla came to the after-school meetings without fail. He was fascinated by his namesake, especially the scientist's later, more crackpot-seeming theories. "I wouldn't spend too much time on those," Martin warned. "It is generally assumed that Tesla made some grand claims that had no scientific basis. He was a little nuts."

"I understand," Tesla said. "But there is a grain of truth to his theories, even if they don't mean what he *thought* they meant."

Martin started to ask Tesla to explain, then realized he had no hope of understanding the Tusker.

Not long after, Tesla stopped coming to class, except on rare occasions.

Another of the brighter students was a female who seemed interested in chemistry and physics. Martin ended up naming her Marie after she became infatuated with Marie Curie. She stopped coming to class about the same time as Tesla, and it eventually became clear to Martin that the two young geniuses were working on a project together.

Then there was Napoleon, whom Martin decided was the smartest of them all. Napoleon could take any historical battle Martin described and immediately break it down into its basic components, reconstructing the fight the way it *should* have happened. Martin found he couldn't argue with him, except to explain that battles weren't always logical, that in the heat of battle, because of the fear and confusion, people did strange and inexplicable things. Napoleon Bonaparte, who according to his namesake had made all the right moves up until the end, fascinated this Tusker.

"The invasion of Russia should have worked," Napoleon pronounced.

"Yes, well, history doesn't always pan out the way you think it will," Martin explained. "People are too complicated. Too many factors come into play."

"Hmmm," Napoleon said, and seemed to think about it for days. Eventually he came back and pronounced, "Never start a land war in Asia or invade Russia in the winter."

"Right," Martin said, almost laughing at how serious Napoleon sounded when he made his pronouncement. It would have been funny, except Martin hadn't taught those two basic truths to the Tusker. Had Napoleon arrived at these conclusions by himself?

So Martin's life might have continued. He was perfectly happy to put in his time teaching the young ones and spend his evenings with his favorites. He felt wanted and content with his life.

Then Genghis showed up one day during one of the

seminars, and sat at the back of the room and watched them for a while. After a stilted beginning, they almost forget their leader was there and had a spirited discussion about the causes of the First World War, Napoleon taking the side of the Germans and Erik taking the side of the Allies.

In the middle of a particularly intense argument, Genghis suddenly rose.

"Good," he grunted in the Tusker language and left, probably not even realizing that Martin had understood him.

The next morning, Martin once again had a crisis of conscience about helping the Tuskers. Was he being a traitor to his own kind? Was he giving these strange creatures the tools they needed to kill humans?

Like Achilles sulking in his tent, he refused to leave his room for a full day. Yet he already knew that the Tuskers could find out most of this information on their own. They didn't need him, except perhaps to provide a human perspective on things. Martin eventually came to the conclusion that he was more likely to sway the Tuskers toward peace by being proactive with them than by keeping to himself.

As if sensing his unease, Napoleon broached the subject at the next seminar.

"We bear humans no ill will," he said quietly. "If it was up to me, we would live in peace. But it is clear from your history that you respect only strength. We must be strong or we will be overwhelmed."

Martin believed him. Perhaps if it had been Gandhi who had tried to reassure him, it wouldn't have had the same impact. But this was Napoleon, who was so smart about tactics that it was frightening.

"But you mustn't fight us," Martin warned. "You cannot hope to win. We have had thousands of years to perfect the art of war."

Napoleon didn't answer. To his surprise, it was Tesla who spoke up. Martin hadn't even realized that Tesla was there, along with Marie. It had been a long time since the two Tuskers had attended the evening conclave.

"I wouldn't be so sure about human invincibility," he said.

"They have great weaknesses that would be extremely easy to exploit. It wouldn't take so much."

"I agree," Marie said. "A few strategic blows and the whole civilization will come tumbling down."

"The Machine will level the playing field," Napoleon said.

"The Machine?" Martin asked, feeling a sudden dread. "What are you planning?"

Marie looked away. "We are only planning for emergencies," she said.

"The trouble with such plans is that they tend to be used," Martin said.

"Don't worry. I will not allow my research to be used unless it is absolutely necessary." Marie looked over at Napoleon uneasily, and Martin had the sudden insight that the other Tuskers—even Marie—tended to be more circumspect whenever Napoleon was nearby.

*What's going on?* Martin wondered. All this time, he'd been worried about the Tuskers' safety. What would happen when humans found them? How would they survive?

Now, for the first time, he wondered if it was the humans who were really in danger.

After Napoleon, Marie, and Tesla left the room, King turned to Martin. "You must be careful with those three," he said. "No matter how they seem, they are not on your side. They are reporting everything to Genghis."

"I assumed that you were *all* reporting to Genghis," Martin said.

"Not always, not anymore," Petunia said. "The more some of us are around humans, the more we doubt that Genghis is correct. We don't believe all humans are evil, or that they mean to exterminate us."

"Napoleon, at least, seems to have doubts," Martin ventured.

"Maybe," Marilyn chimed in. "But he is loyal to Genghis. As are we all, of course, but..."

"Even more importantly," King said, "he is in love with Marie..."

"...and Marie and Tesla are Genghis's favorites," Erik finished for him.

"What is it that they are doing?" Martin asked. "They come into class all covered in oil and grit."

The Tuskers looked at each other uneasily, and then as one, they turned to Goliath, who grunted, "Even I do not know. The south hill is off limits to all but the inner circle. They are building something, something important, but they are not saying what."

From that day on, Martin tried to coax something, anything, from Napoleon about what their project was, but the Tusker was tight-lipped. When Tesla or Marie were in the room, Napoleon turned away as if he hadn't heard the question. When he was alone, he'd simply shake his head and apologize. "I wish I could tell you, Teacher. Hopefully no one will ever have to know."

Those kinds of vague answers turned Martin's mild curiosity into a burning desire to find out the secret.

One day, when Pigstown seemed unusually empty—sometimes the Tuskers were all called together in the Great Hall, and their pet human wasn't invited—he slipped out the entrance of the north hill and walked toward the entrance of its twin companion.

When Martin left the north hill, Goliath followed him. As usual, the human was unaware of being followed. Martin thought Goliath was his friend, but in truth, the huge pig was his guard—or his guardian. Even Goliath wasn't sure which. Not all the glances Martin got from the Kinfolk were friendly. Goliath had stared down a threat more than once.

Goliath watched his teacher with growing disquiet. A strange thing had happened while he accompanied Martin day after day: he'd begun to like the man. And eventually, he'd come to realize he liked all humans and had no desire to hurt them.

Some of their little group agreed with him. Others, like Napoleon and Marie, were conflicted, afraid of humans but not hating them. But all of them knew that their leader Genghis and his immediate circle meant humans ill, and that war was almost inevitable.

*How can you be so naïve?* he wanted to shout at his teacher. *You are betraying your own kind!*

It was Martin's innate decency that had changed Goliath's opinion. The giant pig wasn't as good as some of his Kin at reading human minds, but he'd gotten enough sense of the man to know that he was harmless, and in fact liked Tuskers and wished them well.

Once, Goliath had been part of Genghis's inner circle, but the leader must have sensed something different in his former protégé. He simply couldn't nurture hatred for all humans now that he liked one of them. So Goliath was no longer told everything that was happening. Instead, Tesla and Marie, and especially Napoleon, were now the favorites.

What they were working on was a secret even to Goliath.

Martin crossed the short distance between the hills without being noticed by anyone but Goliath. When the human slipped into a tunnel he'd never visited before, Goliath started to get even more nervous. Even he hadn't been to these sections of Pigstown, understanding without being told that they were off limits. And yet, Goliath was nearly as curious as the human was, and at first he simply followed Martin without trying to stop him.

It was getting hot, and that only seemed to make the human more inquisitive, and he kept going. Finally, Goliath couldn't hold back. He sensed that if either of them were found so deep in the south hill, neither of them would ever leave. He rushed forward, getting ahead of Martin, then turned and confronted the astonished human.

"No go," Goliath grunted, pushing Martin back with his snout.

Martin's face fell, then his jaw set. He ignored Goliath and brushed past him.

"Shit," Goliath grunted, using the human word, and hurried to catch up.

Martin turned a corner, out of Goliath's sight. As he approached a door to the inner chambers, it began to open, and a guard emerged. Martin slid behind the door and managed to catch it before it closed as the guard trotted off.

The door was a duplicate of one that Martin used every day

in the north hill. In fact, most of the rooms in the north hill seemed to be mirrored here, as if they'd been built from the same diagrams. Instinctively, Martin started toward what in his own territory was the Great Hall.

He heard the humming from a long way off. It felt like the entire hill was vibrating. Where he'd expected a doorway, an entire wall had been taken out, as if the machine inside the room had outgrown the space. There was machinery everywhere Martin looked. He slipped to one side of the cavernous space and walked along the edge. A dozen yards in, he was out of the line of sight of the corridor. There, he looked up.

The entire hillside appeared to have been hollowed out, all the way to the top. The machine was a labyrinth of tubes and wires and gears, but it was unlike any machine he'd ever seen. Or rather, it was like the innards of every machine he'd ever seen mashed together. There were liquids dripping, viscous and slow or thin and quick. Sparks flashed between metal spheres, and gears ground at dizzying speeds. Pistons churned and hammers slammed. All of it had a dark, portentous aura, as if just waiting to explode, to destroy everyone and everything.

*The Machine.*

Martin heard someone coming down the narrow, curving path around the machine, and he turned to hurry back to the corridor, but it was too late. Napoleon came into view. He was walking upright and wearing some kind of mechanical gloves on his front hooves. He froze at the sight of the human.

Martin was backing up, and just as he reached the open hallway, Napoleon surged forward. "Get out!" he grunted. "Quickly, before Tesla sees you!"

Martin heard someone behind him and turned with a cry.

It was Goliath. "Follow me!" he rumbled, and turned and ran. This time, Martin obeyed.

They ran down the hallway, the sounds of the machine receding behind them, and yet the vibration stayed with Martin, even as he exited the south hill, even as he entered his own hillside. Even when he reached his room, it seemed to him that everything was vibrating.

Goliath left him at the door. "You must never tell anyone

what you have seen," he warned.

"What *have* I seen?" Martin asked.

Goliath shook his head. "I do not know, but we were fortunate. Napoleon didn't turn us in as I would have expected. Tesla and Marie would have. We may not be so lucky next time."

As Martin tried to sleep that night, he couldn't get his mind off The Machine that filled an entire mountain. The whole scenario was incomprehensible. But certainty suddenly filled him, and he knew that everything that had happened, all his bad luck and bad decisions, had led him to this moment for a purpose.

He didn't know what The Machine was, but he knew it didn't bode well for humanity. It was up to him to warn his people. He began to plan his escape.

# Chapter Eleven

Barry was on the phone moments after Professor Patterson left the barn, demanding to know why the tech guys he had hired—and whom he was paying big bucks—had missed the infestation of javelinas in Utah.

"We wanted to be sure..." Patrick Huskind ventured.

"What part of 'Tell me when you see something unusual' don't you understand?" Barry shouted. He suspected that by the time they waited for absolute certainty, it would be too late.

"There were some anomalies," Patrick said. "We wanted to make sure it wasn't a mistake in the data."

"What kind of anomalies?"

"Well, we saw what appeared to be a large population of the pigs one day, and they disappeared the next—I mean, completely gone. So unless pigs have learned to fly, the first sighting had to be wrong."

Barry closed his eyes and counted to ten. Only he didn't make it. At the count of five, he started talking, his voice rising again. "I'm going to give you my original instructions again. Please let me know when *anything* unusual is happening. I think *anomalies* would qualify as unusual don't you?"

"Yes, sir. I understand."

"Get that information to me as soon as possible, anomalies and all."

"You'll have a report within the hour," Patrick assured him.

Barry hung up and sighed. Maybe it was time to hire some new people—he could even keep Patrick and his crew on, just in case. It was only money, and the money kept rolling in by the second.

He sat back and thought about it, then picked up the phone and called Patrick back. "I want you to investigate a professor of biology at the University of Oregon named Oliver Patterson. Find out what his story is."

"Right away, Mr. Hunter."

When the satellite data showed up on his computer forty-five minutes later, along with it came a slim report on Dr. Patterson. It turned out that although Patterson was a tenured professor, his colleagues didn't hold him in high regard. He was a bit of crypto-biologist, investigating Bigfoot and other mythical creatures in his spare time.

*Just the sort of fellow I ought to have on board,* Barry thought. Though he hadn't liked how the man had tried to extort him.

He picked up the phone before he could change his mind. "Dr. Patterson?" he said when the man answered. He kept the reluctance and distaste out of his voice. "It's Barry Hunter. Would you like to join us on a little field trip to Utah? I'll pay all the expenses."

"You won't buy my silence, Mr. Hunter," Patterson answered pugnaciously. From the sound of the van squeaking and grinding, Barry could tell the man was driving down a bumpy road.

"I understand that," Barry said. "But we are both going in the same direction, and it might be safer if we worked together."

"Safer?"

"Yes, Dr. Patterson. I assure you, safety is something you might want to take into account."

There was a long interval of the van screeching and bouncing, and then Patterson's voice. "I'll be back there by nightfall."

"Good," Barry said. "We'll leave tomorrow morning."

When Flaco's son-in-law first returned from Afghanistan, he seemed fine. Enrique slept a lot, went fishing and rock hunting, and went drinking with his buddies down at the neighborhood tavern.

But then he kept sleeping a lot, and worse, he kept drinking with his buddies.

Flaco tried to interest him in working on the ranch, but both of them knew that wasn't going to happen. Enrique wasn't made for bucking hay or milking cows. Sometimes it seemed like the only thing that kept Enrique coming home at night was Felix. The father and son got along great. Felix lived for the moments when his dad would pick him up and put him on his shoulders, or swing him around like an airplane, or toss him in the air, only to catch him again. The relationship between Alicia and Enrique wasn't so clear. Sometimes the couple was cuddly and affectionate, and other times it was as if they didn't know each other.

Just about the time Flaco was getting concerned enough to say something, Enrique noticed that Flaco was going off at odd times to visit the old Pederson (now Hunter) spread. Flaco couldn't help but be somewhat secretive about it, and Enrique picked up on that right away.

"Why do you go over there?" Enrique asked one day.

Flaco hesitated as he threw his gear into the pickup. "Come with me," he said finally. "I'll show you."

As they drove to the barn, Flaco started to explain about the wild pig infestation that had nearly overwhelmed the valley while Enrique was overseas.

"I thought that was a rabies epidemic," Enrique said.

"That was the official story," Flaco said.

"Were you attacked?" Enrique asked sharply. He seemed more focused than anytime Flaco could remember. He had the sudden insight that this was the way Enrique had been in battle—intense and motivated.

Flaco decided then and there to tell Enrique everything, and more, to involve him in Barry's plans. "Fortunately, I sensed something was wrong," he said. "That was the week I took Alicia and Felix to Hawaii. But I saw the aftermath, and I believe Barry Hunter's story."

"And what was that?" Enrique asked.

Flaco started to tell him, then changed his mind. "Better you hear it from the horse's mouth," he said. "Barry was there, and he is very convincing. And you'll need some convincing, because the story is pretty wild."

Barry gave Flaco an inquiring look when he showed up with Enrique at his side, but by then, Flaco was convinced that involving Enrique was the right thing to do. Maybe it would get his son-in-law out of his funk. Besides, Barry's plans were all about defending themselves, and who knew how to fight better than Staff Sergeant Enrique Flannigan?

Enrique didn't balk once when he was told the entire chronicle of events. He stood up halfway through and started pacing. When Barry was done, Enrique stopped pacing and waved his arms at the reinforced walls of the barn. "Why the fortress?" he demanded. "It sounds like you've already defeated them."

"Well..." Barry said. "One of them...might have gotten away."

"One?"

"Yes, but pigs breed very fast. It's been a couple of years. There could be thousands of them by now."

"But not around here, I take it. I assume you've been watching out for them."

"Of course," Barry said. "But the Tuskers can probably survive anywhere in the Great Basin, or the Great American Desert, as the pioneers called it. Hell, the Tuskers can probably live *anywhere*. Especially if they are as smart as I think they are."

"All right," Enrique said, sitting back down at the table. "Assume I believe you. I will repeat the question, why the fortress? Why would they come back here?"

Barry didn't answer at first, then he looked up with a grim expression. "Revenge. They will come back to finish the job."

"They're animals," Enrique scoffed. "Why would they do that?"

"Animals? That's what you don't understand, Enrique. They are as smart as we are—probably smarter—and every bit as mean and vindictive. I can't tell you how I know they'll be back, but I'm certain of it. Meanwhile, I'm trying to discover where they're hiding. When I find out, I'm going to take the battle to them."

"You and what army?" Enrique asked, amused.

"Well...there's me, and my wife, Jenny, and there's Flaco. And...and I haven't quite worked that out."

Enrique stood up again, but instead of seeming random, his movements now looked precise and calculated, and Flaco had a sudden image of Enrique leading his patrol into enemy territory. "Can I see what's in your gun locker?" he asked, walking over to it.

Barry went over and opened the double doors of the metal locker. Enrique stood in front of the weapons for a few moments, as if he was absorbing the contents, then turned with shining eyes. "You provide the weapons, I can get you your army."

So it was that half a dozen of the men who had served with Enrique in the Middle East came to live at the ranch. They took over the Pederson house, while Barry and Jenny continued to live in the barn. They started working on the ranch, doing all the regular chores, and slowly, they turned the acreage into an armed encampment. It was subtle, but the clues were there if you looked for them.

The veterans regularly practiced target shooting, so Barry wasn't alarmed when he heard a series of gunshots one evening. However, the pattern of the firing was unusual, so he got up from his desk to check it out.

The men had shot a couple of coyotes that had gotten into the chicken coop. (In honor of Lyle Pederson, Barry had kept the livestock, though he wasn't adding to it.) After that, the ranch seemed to be constantly besieged by coyotes. The livestock had to be watched over constantly. Even worse, there was an infestation of ravens. The huge black birds lined the top of the barn and every other manmade structure, cawing constantly, as if bickering among themselves. They'd take flight when the men would fire their guns, but soon enough, they'd be back.

Surprisingly, the veterans paid for themselves in the increased production at the ranch, and eventually, Barry was able to hire almost two dozen men (since they were young, and got somewhat bored waiting for the pigs to show up, their numbers constantly fluctuated), and instead of the ranch costing him money, it started making money, even with the coyote attacks.

*Strange how hard it is to make money when you have none,* Barry thought, *and how easy it is to make money when you already have it.*

When Barry called his troops together to get ready to leave for Utah, Flaco and Enrique showed up an hour later.

"We'll bring Alicia and Felix over to stay with Mrs. Hunter in the barn," Enrique said, taking charge.

"Oh?" Jenny said acidly. "You want to leave all the womenfolk here, because we're so defenseless?"

Enrique looked surprised. "Of course not," he said, frowning. "You can come too, Mrs. Hunter. I just thought…"

Jenny laughed. "It's okay, Enrique. I'm just giving you a hard time. And call me Jenny."

Enrique looked flummoxed, then smiled an embarrassed smile. "I'm not sure why I'm giving orders, actually. Barry is in charge, of course."

"No, no," Barry said, smiling. "That's quite all right. When it comes to military matters, I bow to your expertise."

"It's just that, even though I've shown Alicia how to use a rifle, she doesn't really want to. I'm not sure she'll even remember how to do it."

"Really, Enrique," Jenny said. "Quit apologizing. I was only teasing. I'm content to stay with your wife and child."

"Good," Enrique said, and with civilian matters dispensed with, he was all business again. "We'll take the three Land Rovers," he said. "We have twenty-three men on the premises right now. I'll leave a rear guard of two men and take twenty-one: Flaco and seven of my men in one vehicle, Barry and seven men in another, and me and the rest in the last. It'll be crowded, but I'd rather take too many men than too few."

"We're going to have another member of the party," Barry broke in, explaining that he'd hired Oliver Patterson. "I suspect he'll want to take his own van, however."

"Good. We'll put him in the middle of the convoy," Enrique said. He turned to Barry. "Do you have the coordinates?"

By the time Dr. Patterson showed up that night, they were all packed up and ready to leave the next morning.

# Chapter Twelve

Roger Slawson only made it to his cabin in the Utah mountains once or twice a year, but whenever he did, all the worries and stresses of city life fell away. There was always that moment, a day or so after he arrived, when it was as if a dark cloud lifted from his soul. He'd feel light and pleasantly in the now. Such contentment would wash over him that it would elicit a sigh, and he'd know that he was settled in for his vacation.

*If only I could stay,* he'd think every time it happened. But this time, another thought came. *And why not?*

He was past retirement age. He was wealthy enough to live well in the city, much less in his cabin. He could finally sit down and write the Great Tome that he'd been researching and planning for years. For decades, really. *Why not?*

But he knew that as soon as he drove back to the city, his job would absorb him again, and he'd shrug off his daydreams and get back to work. He needed the ego boost of being the boss. Of ordering people around. Of seeing the revenue come in and knowing it was *his* ideas, *his* inspiration, and most of all, *his* force of will that generated all the money.

Sometimes he wished he could go back to the old days, when he'd been a simple chemist working in a lab. But when his bosses had rejected his formulas once too often, he'd struck out on his own, and when his concoctions had proven to be every bit as effective as he'd thought, he had become the master of a huge corporation, his tinkering days behind him.

The people working for him would be surprised by how crude and unsophisticated the cabin was. Roger could have afforded a nice condo in a millionaires' resort, but he preferred to rough it. That was the whole point: to crank the water up from the well, to boil it on an iron stove with wood he'd chopped himself, to sleep in a rough-planked bed, to shower in cold water, and to hunt for his food.

That's why he was the boss and they were the underlings—because they'd never once in their lives had to rough it. They were never alone with their thoughts. Off the web. Off the beaten track completely.

His cabin sat alone on hundreds of acres of property, at the end of a long and winding and bumpy dirt road. When he'd first bought the cabin, sight unseen from the janitor of the building where he'd first worked, he'd been afraid that, left unattended, it would be broken into. He needn't have worried. If it was far away from civilization, it was also far away from civilization's predators and scavengers.

But not far away from wilderness predators. Roger had made the mistake of leaving food in the cupboards that first winter, and when he'd come back in the spring, he found that a bear had torn off the door and rummaged through the house. It had taken him his entire vacation to put the cabin back in order—which had been incredibly satisfying. He'd been hooked after that, and had resisted making further improvements. He wanted the cabin to be livable, but just barely.

On this trip, the first thing Roger tackled was the outhouse. The hinges on the door had rusted away, and he improvised with some hard leather, creating joints that seemed even tighter than the original metal ones. It was crude but effective, and immensely satisfying. He let out a big sigh.

*There it is*, he thought. *The moment of now.*

He closed the outhouse door and latched it. *What if I never go back?* The business didn't need him anymore. He'd hired enough good people that it was self-sustaining. He'd even begun to suspect that some of his younger employees might have fresher ideas than he did. *Just stay here, never go back.*

He heard a cawing sound and turned to see that the aspen tree that grew near the well was absolutely packed with ravens. Every branch, every square inch of branch, had one of the black creatures on it. As soon as they saw him, they went completely silent and still. It was vaguely creepy and threatening.

Roger waved his arms, but the birds didn't even flinch. He picked up a rock and threw it, and it struck the tree's trunk mere inches from some of the ravens. Still they didn't move.

He heard snuffling behind him. Already spooked, he whirled around and gave a started cry. There was a wild pig watching him, halfway between him and the house.

*That's something new.* He'd heard somewhere that wild pigs were expanding their territory, but he'd never seen one before.

*I wonder what it tastes like?* He eyed the animal. Then he had a strange thought. It occurred to him that the pig was regarding him with the same speculative look.

The thought gave him a bit of a chill. He'd left his rifle propped against the porch railing. If he could somehow avoid spooking the creature and get ahold of the gun, he might have pork for the next few days. Roger was Jewish, but not very observant. He wouldn't ordinarily eat pig, but this was the wilderness, and everything was different out here.

He edged his way to the side of the vegetable garden. (So far, he'd grown nothing edible besides a few small, strange-looking carrots.) The pig turned as he went by, but didn't run away or try to follow him. Roger was so intent on the one pig that he didn't see the passel of them near the porch until it was too late.

At their center was the biggest pig he'd ever seen, even bigger than the porkers he'd once judged at a county fair. Plus, this one was hairy, with red eyes and huge, curling tusks.

But it was the pig's eyes that froze Roger in mid-step.

Roger's forte in business was analyzing the opposition and finding their weakness, the pivot point where he could get what he wanted out of them. In the eyes of this wild hog was the same look he saw in the mirror when he practiced his negotiations, a shrewd and measuring intelligence.

*That can't be*, but his gut told him it was true. In this confrontation, Roger was the weak one, and between him and the rifle that might have equalized them was a foe who meant to kill him.

He raised his hands. "Whoa, fella. I mean you no harm."

The pig snorted, and for all the world, Roger heard in that

snort a cynical dismissal.

"Hey, we can get along. My garden is all yours." He thought furiously. Pigs were omnivores, weren't they? "I've got food inside."

The pig nodded.

Roger had started edging toward the porch again before realizing that he'd read assent in that nod. *Am I going crazy?* he wondered. *Is the isolation making me hallucinate?*

Then again, he'd always believed it was his ability to think for himself that had made him stand out. Once, he'd sat down for a routine negotiation with a young man who owned a much smaller corporation. By the time the meeting was over, Roger had bought the other man's corporation for twice its appraised value—all because he'd seen the enormous potential in the young man. He hadn't been able to keep the guy for more than a few very profitable years, and that man was now one of the richest people in the world. After that, Roger always trusted his instincts.

Roger was halfway up the steps when there was a threatening grunt behind him. He stopped.

The giant pig came up behind him, then brushed past him. It reached the porch and grabbed the rifle in its teeth. It tossed the gun over the railing, where—impossible as it was to believe—another of the porkers took it in its mouth and carried it out of sight.

Roger went inside, leaving the door open, and rooted around for food he could use to bribe his way to safety. He glanced at the knives in the kitchen, but decided against it. He carried an armful of food out to the porch and laid it down.

There on the rough planks was a written message: "Come with us. Or die."

Roger knew his mouth was hanging open. He felt as if every muscle in his body had just given out. He could barely stand. He looked at the giant pig, and again saw that speculative expression.

Roger Slawson, captain of industry, Master of the Universe, friend to the rich and powerful, nodded in acquiescence.

"I'll come. Just don't hurt me."

# Chapter Thirteen

Marilyn had thoughtfully provided Martin with a small table and chair for his meals, brought back from one of the Tuskers' scavenging raids on nearby cabins.

He grunted his thanks for the cooked meat Erik brought him. The Tuskers didn't cook their own food, though he'd tried to convince them that it would free up the nutrients, providing them with more protein.

*Why do I continue to teach them?* he kept wondering. Genghis meant to do humans harm, he was convinced of that. Ever since Martin had found the Tuskers constructing that strange machine, he'd realized that the situation was even more complicated than he'd thought. And little by little, his *favorites* were beginning to confide their doubts to him.

"How does Genghis think he can win?" he asked them, not for the first time. At least, that was what he thought he was saying. He suspected that in Tusker language, it had probably come out something like, "How Genghis win think?"

He continued, "Does he have any idea how many humans there are? How many weapons they have? How practiced they are in the ways of war?"

"He only wants to protect us," Marilyn said.

"Yes, it is self-defense," Erik the Red agreed.

"No," Goliath grunted. The huge Tusker rarely spoke, but when he did, the others always listened, as though they realized Goliath put more thought into his words than any of them. "He *hates* humans."

Martin gnawed on his meat. It was probably rabbit, maybe marmot. Whatever it was, it was gamey-tasting and tough. The

Tuskers didn't quite understand how to prepare meat, and it usually came to Martin either undercooked or overcooked.

King spoke up, though he, too, was usually quiet. "What if we approached the humans? If we could prove to them that we are intelligent, maybe they would accept us. Give us our own place."

"I'm not sure that would be a good idea," Martin said dubiously. "Human history is full of examples of more technologically advanced cultures wiping out or dominating other cultures."

"But we are smarter than humans," Erik said, sounding frustrated.

"Even less reason to let them know you exist," Martin said.

"But we can't hide forever," Marilyn protested. "Some humans already know about us."

"But not for long, if Genghis gets his way," Erik said. "He's getting ready to return to our birthplace and kill all those who opposed us. Then he intends to go into hiding again."

"But why?" Petunia asked. "Why must we kill them? Why can't we just hide?"

"Genghis thinks that if we kill the witnesses," Erik said, "the other humans will be too stupid to realize we exist until it is too late."

"Genghis might be right," Goliath rumbled. "We're growing at an exponential rate. Our intelligence is greater than man's, and we learn faster. If we can remain hidden long enough, we will someday *be* the superior culture."

Martin felt a chill, even as his words rejected the notion. "That seems unlikely," he said. "Humans have satellites. They have all kinds of ways to find us. They are everywhere, and they won't be looking to coexist with a smarter species. They will convince themselves that we are a threat and wipe us out..." His voice trailed off as he realized he was saying "we" and "us." But the others didn't seem to think this was strange.

"I don't think you truly understand the concept of exponential," Gandhi said.

Martin laughed. "I taught it to you. I understand it, but I also know that in the real world, such growth is usually subverted in some way. And growth breeds its own problems, and often its own demise. You Tuskers are unlikely to be left alone long enough to achieve your goals."

"Perhaps," Erik said. "But what choice do we have? We can survive in the wild places where man never goes. Man will not find us. Our numbers will grow and grow, and by the time humanity finds us, it will be too late. If we continue to increase our numbers with every generation, and if we continue to pass on our knowledge, we will soon be far more advanced than mankind."

Martin shook his head. It seemed impossible to imagine. Yet...he'd seen how desolate the wild places in America were. Even more so farther to the north, in Canada. Ranchers had been killing coyotes for generations now, and despite shooting and poisoning and trapping them in huge numbers, there were more coyotes than ever, and they were wilier than ever. Martin laughed as an image of Wile E. Coyote came to him. But was it any more outrageous than pigs with guns?

It somehow seemed appropriate that the coyotes were allies of the Kin—no doubt unreasoning allies, but allies nevertheless—as were the ravens, who Martin had also begun to think of as intelligent. *Are the Kin the only new species? Are these other animals also undergoing a metamorphosis?* He'd watched the coyotes and ravens for a few weeks and decided that they weren't mutants, they were simply under the control of the Kin.

"I don't see why you're laughing," Marilyn said gloomily. "Even if they find some of us, they won't believe we are anything but pigs. They'll kill us, eat us, and never know that they are consuming creatures with souls and intelligence."

While she was speaking, there was a commotion from outside. The Tuskers scrambled from the room, all but Goliath, who was ever faithful to (watchful of?) Martin.

Martin followed them out. He was allowed to wander almost anywhere now, except the south hill, though he tended to stay close to home. Not every Tusker accepted his presence. Some, he suspected, would rip him up one side and down the other with their tusks given half a chance.

One of the Tuskers' patrols was returning, and Martin

couldn't understand what he was seeing at first. He'd been watching Tuskers for so long, communicating with and eating and sleeping around them for so long, that he could almost forget he was a five-foot, ten-inch human being.

The man they were leading into camp was small and dapper, probably in his late fifties or early sixties, with a white beard that tapered to a point and a mustache that curled upward on either end. Whoever he was, he didn't look scared. He looked intrigued. The older man's eyes widened upon seeing another human, and suddenly Martin was aware that he was wearing a dirty T-shirt inside out and ragged shorts that he hadn't bothered to wash in days. The pigs were more fastidious than him.

Martin swallowed his embarrassment and stepped forward with his hand outstretched. "Martin Bleecker," he said.

The newcomer gave him a big smile. "Roger Slawson," he replied, taking Martin's hand and giving it a professionally firm shake. A glimmer of recognition sparked in the back of Martin's mind. No wonder this man looked familiar. The Victorian beard and mustache were his trademark.

"Slawson, as in Slawson Enterprises?" Martin asked.

"That's me," the man said. "How did you know?"

"I spent a week day-trading," Martin said.

"A week?"

"I had five thousand to start, and a week later I had zero."

Slawson laughed. "I hope I wasn't the cause of it."

"No," Martin said. "You were the one bright spot. My mistake was selling."

They stood there awkwardly for a few moments. The pigs had surrounded them and were watching them.

"They understand us, don't they?" Slawson asked quietly.

"Some of them," Martin said. "Most of them, probably. By the end of the week, all of them will, if they think it important enough. They are tremendously smart."

"So I gathered," Slawson said. "I thought it prudent to surrender and offer my services. I assume you had the same experience?"

"I wasn't a volunteer," Martin said. "But...it has been interesting."

"I'll bet."

The big Tusker who had led the patrol grunted "Enough," and Martin nodded. Hercules, as Martin called him, was one of Genghis's main allies. He didn't like humans much.

"You'd better go along with them," Martin said.

"You understand them?" Slawson said, amazed.

"Somewhat. They have their own language, easy to understand, but hard to speak."

"What do they want with me?" Slawson asked over his shoulder as he left.

"I don't know, but whatever it is, I'd advise you to do it."

# Chapter Fourteen

Jenny was both troubled and reassured by the military aspect of the expedition. Enrique Flannigan had automatically taken charge, as usual, and Barry had let him. Since her husband knew what the Tuskers were capable of, he was more than willing to let the experienced soldier lead the way. Besides, most of the men in on the trip were the staff sergeant's old comrades, and they naturally took orders from him.

The second-in-command was a small, quick-moving man named Harrison, a sergeant whose first name Jenny had never heard, who never cracked a smile, and never spoke if he didn't have to. Jenny didn't like him, but figured it wasn't any of her business. The other men seemed to respect him.

Jenny knew Barry would assert himself if he wanted something done. Otherwise, he'd stay out of the way.

"You'll ride in the third SUV," Enrique was telling Dr. Patterson.

"No way," Patterson said. "I'm taking my van."

Enrique eyed the yellow van with its green O dubiously.

"I assure you, young man, this van can go anywhere your Land Rovers can go," Patterson insisted. "I've had it specially outfitted. It's been places you wouldn't believe."

Enrique glanced over at Barry, who shrugged. Then he turned to Harrison, who nodded curtly. "Very well," Enrique said. "But if it breaks down, you better hope we have time to transfer all your stuff. Otherwise, it gets left behind."

"It won't," Patterson said.

Jenny watched the two men's body language and shuddered. Patterson was being condescending to Enrique, calling him *young man* though they couldn't have been that far apart in age. *It's a power struggle,* Jenny decided. The van's big dick against the Land Rover's balls, or something like that. Or perhaps it was the natural conflict of the loner scientist against the soldiers and their teamwork. All Jenny knew was that she was glad she wouldn't have to watch it play out. She was content to stay behind and take care of the homestead.

Patterson slammed the door of his van, as if to make a point, and Enrique stiff-leggedly turned and motioned his men to load up.

Jenny went to the passenger's-side window of the lead vehicle and leaned in to give her husband a kiss. "Don't get into a fight if you can help it," she said. "You'll be in Tusker territory. Who knows what they've come up with?"

"We're just scouting," Barry answered. "Chances are we won't find anything."

"Still," she said, "you've got a small army with you. And armies tend to get used."

"You think maybe I ought to go alone?" he asked, as if he could change things now.

"No, dear. I'd rather you had Enrique and his men along. I just don't want you to get into some battle simply because you can."

He considered that, and it made her heart soften for a moment. He'd always given her opinion respect, never treated her as anything but an equal partner. Even so, they'd started to drift apart when they'd first retired to this Arizona valley, to the point where she'd been ready to get a job just to get out of the house.

The last couple of years had brought them closer again. The danger and their common goal had made them work as a team. Jenny could almost read Barry's mind. He wanted to get the Tuskers taken care of once and for all, but didn't really believe any of them had survived. Jenny had never told him that her own instinct was that not only were there surviving Tuskers, but they were a growing danger. She had no evidence of that— but the Tuskers were too smart not to plan for contingencies.

"Be careful," she said.

Barry nodded to Harrison, and the convoy drove away. It wasn't until they were out of sight that it really hit Jenny. She'd thought she was all right with the scouting expedition, but suddenly she had a bad feeling.

She went into the barn, where the two soldiers Enrique had left behind on guard duty were playing cards. Felix was playing with a big pile of toys that Jenny had bought the previous day while Alicia watched over him. She gave Jenny a nervous smile.

Jenny went to the black spiral staircase that Pederson had installed in the middle of the huge structure and trudged around it to the top, up to the crow's nest and its telescope.

A raven was sitting on the telescope, and it cawed at her defiantly as she reached the platform. She shouted at the creature, which slowly, almost insolently, flapped away, but not before leaving a splatter of white dung on the telescope's casing.

Jenny turned the telescope to the east. She could see the highway, the only road in or out of town, which had been excavated from under the landslide that the Tuskers had set off to isolate the town and repaved with the Pederson money. She watched the convoy climb the slope and then disappear over the top of the hill.

Just as she was about to turn away, she saw movement on the highway below. She squinted, but couldn't see anything. She went back to the telescope and swung it around, scanning the area, trying to pinpoint where she'd seen the movement.

It seemed to her that she saw a shape move into the shadows of the trees, a shape about the size of a dog, but thicker around the chest, with shorter legs. It looked like a javelina, only bigger.

A Tusker…or her imagination, she couldn't be sure.

She saw movement again, and caught a glimpse of several coyotes running across the road. *So that's what I saw,* she thought with a frisson of relief. And yet…she wasn't quite sure.

Jenny went back down the stairs and over to the gun locker, and took out the semi-automatic she'd been training with. The two men playing cards noticed and stood up. She nodded toward the crow's nest, and one of them nodded back, went to the stairs, and quickly climbed up.

With the gun close at hand, Jenny sat down next to Alicia

and watched Felix try to build a tower of blocks bigger than he was. It kept toppling over, much to his disgust and to Alicia's gentle laughter.

Jenny suddenly doubted that what she had seen at first had been coyotes. The image in her memory was of a large, round shape—something like a pig. But if so, why had a Tusker suddenly appeared right as Barry and most of the men were leaving?

It was almost as though the creature had been on watch.

Which meant the Tuskers knew that most of the men on the ranch had headed in the direction they thought the Tuskers were hiding.

And which meant the Tuskers might know the valley had been all but stripped of its defenders.

Jenny got up and quietly closed the barn door, and after a moment, bolted it.

Alicia was setting at the table, her cellphone to her ear. "I want you to call me every hour," she was saying. Enrique must have agreed, for her face lit up. "I love you too, honey."

Jenny almost asked for the phone, to inform Enrique and Barry that she'd—perhaps—sighted a Tusker. She decided against it. No sense worrying the men until she was certain.

# Chapter Fifteen

Sometimes, Bart Hoskins could almost forget finding what was left of his neighbor's body in the backyard. At least, it was assumed that it was Jerry Harper he'd found. There had mostly been only pieces of him, his red, glistening guts spread out on the immaculately green lawn, his severed arms and legs forming an almost geometric pattern. His head was never found. The lawn mower had been going in circles around his body, unattended.

Bart had retreated to his home, turned out the lights, and waited out the javelina apocalypse, which his poker pals were jokingly calling the Aporkcalypse. If not for Lyle Pederson's visit in the midst of it all, asking him to notarize a change in his will that left his estate to Jenny and Barry Hunter, the banker might have believed the official story about rabid pigs.

But Lyle had been the smartest man Bart had ever met, and he'd seemed both scared and determined.

Bart watched with interest as the Hunters continued to fortify their inherited ranch after Lyle's death. It wasn't as if he had much else to do. He had thought for a time, before the Aporkcalypse, that his partnership with the real estate agent Peter Gandry might make him rich. But it had all depended on getting one of the two large landowners in the valley, either Lyle Pederson or Flaco Morales, to let loose some of his excess land.

With Peter gone (they never did find his body, though the Hunters had reported seeing him killed), it was all moot. Both the Hunters and the Morales's had made it clear that no more land would become available for real estate development.

That meant Bart was back to being a small-town banker, as boring as that was.

Still, he didn't mind. He'd come to realize that he'd survived a very dangerous episode, and suddenly just being alive and unhurt was enough.

The height of his week nowadays was having his buddies over for poker night—or rather, poker afternoon, since they were all getting so old and fuddy-duddy that they'd be half comatose if they waited too late in the evening to get started. So they usually kicked things off around five o'clock, and the last of them, usually the druggist, Johnny Olsen, would wander off around nine-ish. Johnny lived right down the street, so it was all right that he drank more than the rest of them; he was immensely boring sober and immensely entertaining drunk.

It just so happened that the same group of men was most of the members of the Saguaro City Commission, which was why the beer could be written off as *refreshments*. The only one who wasn't there was the mayor, Herb Jensen. It wasn't that he was blackballed, it was just that none of them invited Herb, who tended to be self-important and bombastic and wasn't much fun to be around.

It was an unwritten rule that they wouldn't talk business during the game; that was saved for the once-a-month half-hour meeting in the back room of the bank.

None of them spoke much about the Aporkcalypse, though when he drank enough beers, Johnny could be coaxed into going on about it. Like now, for example.

"Talked to any pigs lately?" Harvey Johansson asked him. The hardware store owner had been out of town that week and had come home to a store that was wiped out of guns, ammo, and survival supplies. ("Best week I ever had," he'd said once, but in a subdued tone, since his manager, Joe Sanders, and one of his employees, Mark McCallister, had been killed in the rampage.) Harvey loved needling Johnny and getting him talking, usually around beer number four or five.

"I'm telling you," Johnny said, not at all abashed, "the pig looked right at me and said, 'You're next.'"

The men guffawed, as usual, but Bart always thought there

was a tone of discomfort under all the laughter. All of those who had been through the Aporkcalypse had seen things that weren't natural.

"I've taken to shooting every javelina I see," Fred Carter said. The rancher lived farther out of town than the rest of them. "Fuck the little bastards."

"Not like there is an animal control officer around to stop you," Anthony Lawrence said. He had inherited the local McDonald's from his parents and was richer than all the rest of the men at the poker table combined.

"Are they ever going to replace Hamilton?" Johansson asked.

"I heard they've pawned the job off on the county sheriff," Lawrence said.

"Lot of good the deputies did for us last time," Johnny groused. The Sheriff's Office was located in the next town over, and when the landslide had buried the highway, the people of the valley had been on their own except for one deputy, who had been taken out by the explosion at the Silverstein house. Since then, the residents of Saguaro had insisted on a sheriff presence in the Morrow Valley, and they had set up a branch office in the courthouse.

"So you want to hire our own policeman for the town?" Carter asked. "Good luck trying to get that funding measure passed."

"Oh, I don't know," Bart said. "I think people might just be scared enough this time."

They fell silent at that. They all knew what he was talking about, and they were the movers and shakers who could get it done.

But not on poker night.

"Deal me out for a couple hands," Bart said. "I need a smoke." He pulled his chair back and walked to the sliding door to his patio. As he opened the door, he heard Johansson say, in a conspiratorial sotto voce tone, "All right. Whenever Bart raises, we all call him, OK?"

Bart glanced back and rolled his eyes at their grins, then closed the screen door behind him. He sat on the lawn chair and lit up.

He was building a fence around his yard, six feet tall and solid. But it was only half done, and Bart still made sure all his windows and doors were locked at night. He glanced over at his neighbor's small fence, which hadn't been sufficient to keep Jerry Harper's porcine killer out.

Despite all his caution, the javelina was at the edge of the patio before Bart saw him. He caught the movement out of the corner of his eye, turned his head, and froze.

The pig was staring at Bart. He was huge, twice as big as most javelinas, and had long, curved tusks, unlike the short, straight ones of the native peccaries. Bart had overheard Barry Hunter talking to his wife about this new breed of pigs during one of the hearings about Pederson's will. Hunter had called them Tuskers and had implied they were something special, some kind of mutants.

Bart had no doubt about that. He laughed along with the others when Johnny described the talking pig, but he'd also seen the Tuskers, and he'd known they weren't mindlessly rabid, but deadly, malevolent, and calculating.

Bart got up slowly and started sliding the patio door open. The pig didn't move, as if realizing he couldn't attack in time. It seemed to Bart that the Tusker was almost amused.

*"You're next,"* he remembered Johnny mentioning the pig had said. Suddenly it didn't seem strange at all that the man had thought he'd heard a pig speak.

Bart slipped into the house, slid the door shut, leaned against the glass, and closed his eyes.

He sat back down at the table. The others were having such a good time, they didn't seem to notice his change of mood. When he absentmindedly raised a bet, they all shouted in unison, "We call!"

Bart didn't crack a smile.

He flipped his cards onto the table. "You've wiped me out. Say...you know, it's really early yet. Have any of you guys been over to the Pederson spread since Barry Hunter took it over?"

Johnny was immediately interested. "I've been wanting to see that place. It looks like it could hold off a Panzer division."

"Yeah, what's the story with that?" Lawrence chimed in. "Who the hell are the Hunters, and why did Pederson leave his ranch to him?"

"I'm sorry, guys," Bart said. "Privileged information. I can't talk about it."

Carter laughed. "So here's what you do. If we guess right, you don't say anything. Okay?"

Bart was silent, which only seemed to encourage his friend.

"I've heard the Pederson was filthy rich," Carter said. "Is that true?"

Bart was trying to think of what to say or not to say, and the others suddenly looked intrigued, as if what had started as a joke had become an opportunity to learn something.

"I heard he was the cause of the rampage," Johansson said.

"No way," Bart said.

"But he seemed better prepared than the rest of us," Carter said.

"He was one smart man," Bart said. "Come on, let's go for a visit. I'm sure Barry won't mind. I move that we adjourn and visit the Pederson/Hunter ranch to make sure it is up to code. All in favor?"

"Aye!" they all said, standing up as Carter, the big winner for the night, scooped up his poker winnings while the losers tried to ignore him.

They made their way to the front door, trying to figure out whose vehicle to take. In the end, they all took their own vehicles, and Johnny rode with Bart. After they pulled up in front of the Hunter barn less than five minutes later, they gathered together, as if suddenly uncertain about whether they should descend en masse on the Hunters without warning.

The ranch, which was usually bustling with activity, was strangely quiet. Even eerier, on top of the barn was a line of silent ravens that extended onto the wires leading to the generator shed a hundred feet away.

"*Caw!*" Johnny shouted, as if it was a joke. But nobody was laughing, neither human nor raven.

"Thing is," Johansson said quietly. "The Hunters never stopped fortifying after the Porkocalypse. Makes you wonder what they know that we don't."

*Precisely,* Bart thought. *And I'm going to find out tonight, one way or the other.*

# Chapter Sixteen

"You gonna have dinner ready this time?" Gary Sweeter asked as he headed out the door. Exactly what he did all day wasn't clear. There was nothing but high desert in every direction. He'd get in his battered pickup, drive over the horizon, and disappear for hours on end.

Bridget Colter's heart sank at the disdainful tone in his voice. Things had started out so well. He'd been in such a good mood driving to his cabin, and then the second he closed the door behind them he turned into someone else.

His letters from prison had been so chatty, so interesting, so...evolved. Bridget had offered to teach an online writing course for the prisoners, and Gary's efforts had been, by far, the best she'd seen. He was a better writer than she was, frankly. He had problems with spelling and grammar but his stories were so brutally real.

He'd acted grateful in the beginning, right up to the point when she'd picked him up at the prison gates. But since they had arrived at the cabin, he hadn't said three words to her that weren't a demand. Even the sex was perfunctory, as if she was nothing more than some kind of receptacle. Actually, that had been exciting at first, but now it was getting old. A little, tiny bit of tenderness would be nice.

*Dinner? How am I supposed to make dinner with the supplies I have?* It wasn't possible, but the last time she'd said that, Gary's hand had whipped out and smacked her cheek, and he'd leaned into her face and shouted, "Make me a fucking meal, bitch!"

"It'll be ready for you," she said as cheerfully as she could.

Bridget sat down the moment the door slammed and put

her head down on the table. She'd lost at least ten pounds from her pudgy body since they'd arrived two weeks ago, which normally would have been a cause for celebration. But the fat seemed to have gone from all the wrong spots—not from her tummy or her double chin, but from her arms and legs, where she least needed to lose it. It made her all spindly looking.

She went through the cupboards. Canned peas, tuna fish, some tomato sauce. Maybe she could make some kind of casserole. She'd have to go outside and find some wood for the stove.

Bridget was a city girl. She couldn't sleep at night because of the intense quiet, broken only by Gary's snoring. She'd never cooked anything on a wood-burning stove before in her life, and the first few meals had been overcooked on the outside and undercooked on the inside, and Gary had been even meaner than usual after that.

*I should leave*, she thought, lifting her head. But she didn't really even know where she was. She'd made the mistake of napping during the last few hours of the car trip. The last town she could remember going through was Provo, Utah, but they could be just about anywhere in Utah or one of the neighboring states.

If she walked down the dusty road, she was more likely to see Gary coming toward her than to find anyone else.

Wherever Gary went down that long road and over the horizon had alcohol, though Bridget couldn't figure out where he was getting the money for it. She had seen his fat wallet on the dresser, twenty-dollar bills bulging out the sides, and she was pretty sure that it had been much thinner when they'd arrived. In spite of all his pretty promises to stay straight ("With you helping me, baby, I'm sure I can do it!") she was certain he wasn't on the up and up.

The other night, he had come home reeking of a new scent, and Bridget had cried herself to sleep (the first night they hadn't had sex) with the smell of another woman's perfume filling the bedroom.

Gary was getting meaner and meaner with every passing day, every hour, every minute.

But if she left, then what? Return to her one-room apartment and get another retail job, her only communication with her fellow man the chitchat she could coax from strangers at the counter? Go back to writing letters to thieves and murderers in prison, and sending them ten-year-old pictures of herself?

Bridget found enough wood to cook the casserole. It was pretty bad. It turned out that tomato soup was no substitute for mushroom soup when it came to a tuna dish, but it was too late to cook anything else. Gary usually got up after noon and returned home sometime after dark, which was only an hour or so away.

Bridget would have to try to keep the dish warm, but she was out of wood. She put on a coat and some boots over her nightgown. The one advantage to living without neighbors was that she didn't have to get dressed to go outside.

There was an axe near the shed, but it scared her. So far, she'd been willing to range pretty far to find small branches and twigs. She heard Gary's pickup coming down the road and hurried to fill her arms with wood, but he arrived before she could get to the door.

"What the fuck are you doing, woman?" he said, sauntering over to her.

Bridget's heart fell. He looked angry about something, and the last time that had happened, he'd been verbally abusive, even more than usual, calling her a prison whore and a slut.

"You want wood, you chop it," he said, walking over to the stump with the axe embedded in it. He grabbed a large piece of wood from the pile near the shed, set it down on the stump, and wobbled the axe head down on it. The axe glanced off the wood and swung toward his legs, missing him by inches.

Bridget restrained a cry.

"Shit," he muttered. He tried again, and this time the axe cut the wood cleanly. "See?" he shouted triumphantly. "That's how you do it!"

Bridget cried out and let the kindling fall with a clatter. Gary looked up, to see she was staring at something behind him.

There were three javelinas standing only a few feet away, at the edge of the shed.

"What are you scared of, Bridget?" Gary asked. His voice had taken on the Southern drawl he affected when he was drunk. "Why, these ain't nothin' but little piggies..."

As he uttered the word *little*, a fourth pig revealed itself. This one was massive.

Gary took the axe in both hands and raised it over his head. "Get the fuck out of here, you fucking pigs!"

He swung down at the nearest javelina, who easily dodged. The axe sank into the ground and must have hit a rock. Bridget saw Gary's arms stop with a jolt and heard a loud clank. Before he could raise the axe again, the three smaller animals darted forward and swirled around his legs. Gary cried out, clapped his right hand over his shin, and then toppled over onto his butt.

"Get the rifle!" he screamed at Bridget, but she didn't know what he was talking about. She'd never seen any guns in the cabin.

"In the pickup, you stupid bitch!"

She started backing up toward the pickup, but the huge pig trotted over, almost casually, and stood between her and the truck.

Meanwhile, the javelinas continued to circle Gary, darting in at him whenever he turned away. He had dropped the axe and was holding his wrist, blood spurting between his clenched fingers. "Jesus, these fuckers are cutting me!" he shouted. "Get the goddamn gun, Bridget!"

She and the enormous pig stared at each other, and it seemed to her that the animal shook its head in warning.

Gary cried out again behind her, and Bridget turned to see that he was now on his back, holding his arms over his head as the smaller pigs kept charging him. He grunted, once, twice, and then his whole body stiffened and he let out the strangest sound. Then he relaxed and lay back as if he was sleeping.

A pig shot forward, lunging toward his neck, and a fountain of blood sprayed out, first pumping out in spurts, propelled by his fast-beating heart, then more slowly and in smaller jets. Finally, with a gurgling sound like the last of the water going down a partly clogged drain, Gary went completely still.

Bridget turned and ran for the cabin, and heard the giant

pig clambering up the steps behind her. She slammed the door just as something struck the other side with a thud.

*Safe*, she thought. *Safe.*

But the doorknob started to turn. She watched it in horrified fascination, unable to move. There were knives in a drawer only a few feet away, but she'd forgotten about them. When they had first arrived, she'd almost been unable to turn that knob, it was so rusty. It was easier after a couple of weeks of use, but still…it was impossible that an animal could turn it.

The door swung open and the huge pig stood there, reared up on its hind legs. It had some kind of mechanical gloves on its front hooves.

Bridget's legs gave out. By luck, one of the chairs at the kitchen table was right behind her. She landed on it awkwardly, but caught her balance before falling over completely. The pig removed the gloves and put them in a pack that Bridget only now noticed it was wearing near its hindquarters.

It walked over to her, and she held her breath. She almost fainted before she remembered to inhale again. The pig raised its front legs and propped itself on the table. It stared at the sheets of paper that Bridget had been using for writing letters and grunted.

It dug its snout back into its pack and awkwardly stuck a hoof into one of the mechanical gloves again. Then, almost delicately, it picked up the pen and started writing.

*This isn't happening*, Bridget thought. *Gary's given me a concussion or something, or I'm still back in my apartment and this is all a dream.*

The pig finished scratching and turned the page so that she could see it. "Please come with me. I will not hurt you. We need your help."

Bridget couldn't make sense of the words at first, and then a thought struck her. *When was the last time anyone asked for help from me?* And then, as a strangely warm glow replaced her fear. *When was the last time anyone said "Please"?*

# Chapter Seventeen

Bridget had been with the Kinfolk, as they called themselves, for several weeks before she knew that any other humans were in the settlement. When she found out, she felt an unreasoning jealousy. She had thought she was the only one, and therefore important.

"We need your help," the Great One had written when she was brought into his presence. Right away, she had realized he was special. It was as if he could read her mind, as if he understood her.

"You should have asked first," she'd said with her last ounce of pride. These animals had killed Gary. She couldn't forget that, no matter how much of a jerk he had been. Yet they had treated her with nothing but kindness. And Gary had attacked them with an axe, after all. The Kinfolk had a right to defend themselves, didn't they?

The Great One had gazed upon her with kind eyes. "I am sorry," he wrote. "You are allowed to leave at any time. My name is Genghis. My Kin did not follow my orders."

Bridget was instantly mollified. She didn't want to leave. Where would she go?

"Why did you bring me here?" she had asked.

"The humans would not understand if they knew about us. They would kill us. Indeed, they have already tried. I was the only survivor of my family."

"I'm sorry," Bridget had said, for she could see the animal was in pain.

"I do not wish my Kinfolk to suffer the same fate."

"What do you need?" she'd found herself saying, somewhat to her own surprise.

"There are places we cannot go without revealing ourselves. We need someone to bring back things from human domains. Would you help us? Please? We want only peace, but we cannot survive without help."

It was the kindness in his eyes that had won Bridget over. "Of course I will help you. Humans can be mean."

"Yes," the Great One had agreed.

Bridget had looked at the blank slate and realized that Genghis had spoken English. She'd stared at him with wide eyes.

"I knew you would understand," the pig had said.

Her audience over, she'd been escorted to a small room inside one of the cliffs, which was furnished with blankets and several small pieces of furniture. She'd wandered out and about, and none of the Kinfolk stopped her from moving around. She'd even left the camp and traipsed down the road for several miles to see what the Kinfolk would do. They'd kept an eye on her, but made no move to stop her. As far as she could tell, she was free.

That night, she returned in time for the evening meal.

Bridget soon started making friends. She met Blake and Keats and Byron, sensitive pigs all. She found that they loved romantic poetry as much as she did. She began to think of them as almost human.

It was on her third trip back to the camp (she'd been supplied with a nice SUV, a better vehicle than she had ever driven before) that she saw the two men. They stared at her, and she stared back at them. The younger of the men, a nerdish-looking guy, raised his hand in greeting. The older man just frowned.

She waved back, but her friends Keats and Byron seemed to be in a hurry to meet with Genghis, so she followed them. Later, when she went looking for the men, she couldn't find them.

"Who are they?" she asked Blake, the Kin who always seemed to be with her. She thought he liked her.

"They are not important," Blake wrote. "They stumbled upon us, and we could not let them leave. They do not understand us the way you do."

"They are prisoners?"

Blake hesitated before scratching out, "They are guests. We treat them with kindness."

Bridget nodded. Of course they did. She could only imagine how hard it must be to be nice to people who wanted to kill you. She decided she would stay away from the men. She liked the Kinfolk so much better.

They reached her room, and Blake left her. Making sure that there was no one in the tunnel outside, she removed the little radio she'd bought with the money Genghis had given her. She'd lied and told the Kinfolk that things had cost more than they really did.

Bridget's first job for the Kin had been to convert gold into money. She'd ranged all over the state to do so, and toward the end, she had started getting inquiring looks from the jewelry stores and pawn shops where she sold the nuggets. Once, she had even been followed by a couple of grizzled old men, whom she had heard talking to the clerk earlier about their mining claim.

They had almost reached the settlement when she'd seen their car, behind her, veer off the road. She'd stopped, gotten out, and looked back, trying to see through the dust. She had thought she heard screams and shuddered. Then she'd gotten back in the SUV and driven the rest of the way home.

When she told the Great One about that, he'd told her that they had enough cash and that he now needed her to buy supplies.

Strangely, what they wanted her to pick up were simple things: electrical components and batteries from Radio Shack, simple tools from hardware stores, and some over-the-counter medications from drugstores. Things that any human could have bought any day.

Bridget had no idea what the Kinfolk needed these things for, but it went to show how smart they were that they'd managed to create this little paradise all by themselves. These pigs—no, she wouldn't call them that—these Kin were nicer and gentler than any humans she had ever known.

Roger Slawson screamed as Brutus applied the red-hot iron rod to his chest. Screaming helped, as did swearing, as did crying.

At first, he'd been stoic, but then he'd realized that it didn't matter. The only ones to witness his shame were his torturers. It was a soundproof room, he realized. They didn't want the other humans in the encampment to hear his cries.

Torture had come last. They'd tried everything else first. They had bunked him with Martin Bleecker in the beginning, and some of the pigs that Martin had named, Petunia, Erik the Red, Marilyn, and Goliath. The big pig was the brains of the little group, Roger realized with the same intuitiveness he had always brought to business. People often mistook being big and slow for being dumb, but Goliath was anything but dumb. Roger had caught the cold, calculating look in the pig's eyes when Goliath thought he wasn't looking.

Martin seemed oblivious. He liked the pigs. It was all Roger could do not to accuse his new friend of being a quisling.

The Tuskers had tried to coax Roger at first, then to persuade him, then had started making demands and threats, but he could see through their ploys and wasn't about to give up the information they wanted. Surprisingly, they already had ninety percent of the formula. The part they were missing was the most essential and the most unexpected, one that Roger himself had only stumbled across by accident: a substance that was readily available, but that only Roger had been smart enough to try. There were a couple of chemicals in there that no one had been able to guess or to reverse engineer. The combination of ingredients, most of which were simple household products, had made him rich. To this day, no one really knew the exact formula but him.

When the Tuskers saw that he wasn't going to give in, they removed him from Martin and his companions and handed him over to Brutus, Cassius, and Cato. Roger had decided to name the pigs after Romans. Genghis, for instance, should have been named Caesar, although with his Fu Manchu mustache, the Asian name was understandable.

Brutus and Cassius were thugs; Cato was in charge. Cato made no pretense of being a friend. He was there to extract from Roger the name of the final chemical in the formula, by any means possible.

Roger was determined to die first. He'd heard that no one

could resist torture forever. Well, he didn't believe that. He was going to prove that wrong.

The pain was so intense that Roger was blurting out something, he wasn't sure what. He only knew he hadn't given them what they wanted, because they continued the torture.

Finally, they left him. They took the lanterns with them. He sat in the dark, strapped to the chair, and as bad as the pain was, it was the lack of water that tormented him most of all. *Just one sip of water,* he thought feverishly. *Just one.*

Lights filled the room. Roger awoke, amazed that he'd fallen asleep. The pain came back, a hard throb instead of a lightning bolt, but somehow worse in that it wouldn't go away.

Genghis was standing in front of him, accompanied by his full entourage of bodyguards and underlings. "You must give us the formula," he said, or rather, commanded to be written.

"No," Roger said.

Genghis nodded to one of his underlings, who came forward with a handful of tablets, on which were written a series of equations. The pig held up each of the plaques, one by one.

Roger's heart dropped further upon recognizing each formula. They had them all. All the deadly gasses mankind had ever created. Nerve gas, mustard gas, anthrax, and some he had never even heard of, but which, from his knowledge of chemistry, he understood to be equally deadly.

"These are the formulas we can and will use, if you do not give us yours," Genghis said.

Roger hung his head. His formula was designed not to kill, but to incapacitate. It wasn't an easy thing to knock people out without killing them. If they fell a certain way, if their breathing was impeded, if they were allergic to something in the gas; all these things could be fatal. And a certain percent died simply from being gassed, just as a certain percent of patients in surgery or in the dental chair died from anesthesia.

Roger's formula had been tested and retested, and miraculously, it was the one knockout gas that seemed one hundred percent safe, outside of freak accidents. It spread farther and faster than any other formula. If it were released from high ground, it would spread out below for miles and miles. It was a military secret because it was so effective.

Genghis had him. Roger didn't doubt for one second that the pig would use the deadlier alternatives if he wasn't allowed the safer chemical.

"Sodium hydrogen carbonate," he muttered.

Genghis grunted something, and his scribe furiously scribbled with his gloved hoof.

"This is your last chance. We will use nerve gas if we must."

"No," Roger said. "It's true! $NaHCO_3$."

Genghis spoke, and his translator couldn't help but show his incredulity. "Baking soda?"

"Baking soda, a one percent solution, added at the end. That's all you need. That's all you're missing."

The pigs left the room, leaving Roger in the dark, alone with his doubts.

When Cato and his confederates came for him, Roger wasn't sure what to expect. Now that they had what they wanted from him, there was nothing to keep them from getting rid of him.

They handled him brusquely, but not without some care, and dragged him back to Martin's room and laid him on the bed.

When Martin returned later that night, he took one look at Roger, cried out, and rushed to his side. Petunia and Marilyn stood nearby, and they gave a series of grunts.

Martin looked surprised. "They say, 'This is wrong. This must not be allowed.'"

Roger grunted, a human-sounding grunt, but readily understandable by both species. "Good luck telling Genghis that. I don't think he cares what Petunia thinks."

The two pigs grunted some more, and Martin listened.

"Not everyone believes Genghis is right," Martin translated. "It is time we met the opposition."

# Chapter Eighteen

As usual, Blake escorted Bridget to the road where the SUV was parked. It was about an hour hike, and they made it in silence, companionably. She hopped into the front seat and drove away with a cheery wave.

She hadn't spotted the other two humans even once since the first time she'd seen them.

"They are not our friends," Genghis had said.

"But maybe I can convince them," she'd said. Despite her newfound friends, better friends than she'd ever had, Bridget was hankering for some human contact, someone to talk to, at least.

But when Genghis turned down her offer to talk to the men, she didn't press the issue.

On this trip, Bridget went to every shop in town that sold baking soda and loaded the back of the SUV with it. What Genghis wanted with that much baking soda, she couldn't imagine. The clerks gave her some strange looks, but she laughed as she added a few gallons of vinegar to her purchases, and told them that her daughter was building a giant volcano for science class. That seemed to satisfy them.

"I'd like to see that one go off!" one of them commented after loading several dozen boxes of baking soda into shopping bags.

As Bridget started driving back to the Kinfolk encampment, it occurred to her that she had an SUV with half a tank of gas and a couple of hundred dollars left over. She could just keep driving, straight out of the state, back to her mother's house.

It would be a final defeat.

She'd spend the rest of her life taking care of her mother, Beverly, and listening to her mother tell her what a failure she was.

"You want to be a writer?" Beverly had exclaimed when Bridget had left home. "Fine. But you better have a real job first."

"You've never thought I could be a writer, but I'm going to prove you wrong."

Beverly's last words to her had been, "You are soft-headed. You let people use you, and you're grateful for it. Try to be a little more suspicious."

*I can't live that way,* Bridget thought. *I have to depend on my instincts.*

The Kinfolk needed her and trusted her, and she thought they even liked her. When had she ever been able to say that about anyone?

No, she'd see it through. Be a faithful friend. Help them survive.

And she'd have a story to tell that was worth writing about.

Every few days, Genghis gathered his followers and chose one of them to become a messenger, a vanguard of the Kinfolk. He would call the Chosen forward and give the Kin instructions: over time, this developed into a ceremony.

"Go forth," he would grunt. "Find a place of refuge. Seek out the lesser Folk and join them, and raise your families. Find the Brethren Ravens and Coyotes. Gather them and turn them to our cause. Wait for my signal, for the Day of Retribution will soon be at hand, when we shall take back the Earth from the human interlopers."

The Kin would be shown a map of where to go, and given a single coyote companion and a mated pair of ravens.

At first, the Chosen had been graduates of Martin's school, and he had been allowed to observe the ceremonies (which gathered more pomp and significance with every passing month). Then the Kin had been pigs that Martin had never met, and eventually, he was no longer asked to attend. Then he wasn't even told about the ceremonies at all.

So he could only guess how many of these scouts had been

sent out, but it had to be in the hundreds by now. When he started doing the math on how many litters were being born throughout the continental U.S., it gave him pause. Once again, he started to have doubts about whether he should be helping the Kin at all.

*But in some ways,* he thought, *this rebellion by the wild creatures of the world is mankind's fault. It's only what we deserve. We created the conditions where animals had to evolve to survive. We have tried to murder Mother Nature, and she's fighting back.*

What gave him hope were his companions, Petunia, Erik, and Marilyn. Barry still wasn't quite sure about Goliath.

The huge pig was following Barry and Roger and the others into one of the back storerooms. Roger must have been more injured than he'd let on, because halfway there, he stumbled. Goliath put his massive back under Roger's right hand, and the human leaned on the giant pig the rest of the way.

It was quiet in the tunnels. They didn't run into anyone else. Genghis and most of the Kinfolk were outside, at a Ceremony of Leave-taking, as they were calling them now.

When they got to the storeroom, Martin sat on a case of baking soda, of all things, and waited for Erik to speak.

"The war has begun," Erik said bluntly.

"What do you mean?" Martin asked.

"I have learned that Genghis has already sent an army of Kinfolk back to Genesis Valley," Erik said.

"Genesis Valley?"

"The place of our origin," Erik answered. "You humans called it the Morrow Valley, in the state of Arizona."

"He did this without conferring with anyone," Marilyn said. "Including the second-generation Kin in this room. He has become more and more dictatorial and will not listen to anyone's advice. I believe that he means to start a war with the humans, and I do not believe we can win it."

Petunia spoke up. "It doesn't matter whether we succeed or not. War is wrong. Too many will die for no good reason. I understand that we must hide, I understand that we must defend ourselves, but I do not agree with the idea of wiping the humans out."

"I doubt Genghis believes he can do that," Marilyn said. "I believe he wants revenge, and he wants to send a warning to the humans to leave us alone."

"That's not what will happen," Roger Slawson said. "Even if he succeeds in killing a large number of humans, he is miscalculating the reaction. The more he kills, the more extreme the reaction will be."

"What do we do?" Martin asked.

"We should send a messenger to the humans in that valley," Roger said. "Warn them of what is about to happen."

"We already thought of that," Marilyn said. "Gandhi and King and some of the others who believe as we do will follow the war party. We hope they will find a way to stop them. But there are not enough of us to confront Genghis directly. All we can do is observe."

"Observe?" Roger's voice was low and intense at first, but with each word, it rose. "Observe? You have to do more than *observe*!"

They fell silent at that, and all eyes turned to Goliath, as if they all understood that the massive pig's approval was needed before anything else could be done.

Goliath grunted. "Agreed. The humans must be warned. They must be told that not all Kin wish to kill them. Otherwise, I believe the Kinfolk will be hunted to extinction."

"Then you'll have to get us out of here," Roger said. "We are the only ones who can convince the human authorities of the threat. You wouldn't get near anyone in a position of power. I, on the other hand, know people who can help us."

"We will go with you, as witnesses," Petunia said.

"We must leave as soon as possible," Erik said. "Before the fighting begins."

They all turned to Goliath, waiting for instructions.

"I will stay," he rumbled. "I am the one who reports to Genghis. I will try to conceal your absence for as long as possible."

They had started to discuss how and when to leave the caves when Martin spoke up. "We can't leave without the woman," he said.

"What do you mean?" Petunia asked.

"There is a woman in camp," Martin said. "Roger and I saw her. We have to take her with us."

"We don't have time," Petunia exclaimed.

"I don't care," Martin said stubbornly. "I'm not leaving without her."

"I know where she is," Erik said. "One of my brothers is watching her. He says she is doing Genghis's bidding."

"Perhaps she's afraid, and being coerced," Martin said. "Anyway, we have to give her a chance to come along."

"I agree," Erik said. "Genghis might take out his anger on her. We can't let that happen. I will go get her and bring her here."

Again, they all looked to Goliath, who was still and quiet for a long time, staring at the ground. Then he let out a grunt of assent. "But you must leave tonight," he said. "I will try to assign the guards in such a way that you will have a clear escape. At midnight, leave by the south route. You have until daylight before I will be unable to conceal your absence, so don't linger. Hurry to the first town you find."

Erik left the storeroom, followed shortly afterward by Goliath. The others sat and planned their escape. They decided they would bring nothing along and wouldn't even return to their rooms. They would leave with only what they had.

"What about guns?" Marilyn asked.

"I will not fire on my Kin," Petunia said. When no one disagreed with her, the idea was dropped.

A few minutes later, the woman entered the storeroom, followed by Erik.

Martin hopped off the case of baking soda and extended his hand. "Martin Bleecker," he said. "And this is Roger Slawson. We are fellow prisoners here."

The woman seemed surprised. She hesitated, then shook his hand. "Bridget Colter," she said.

"We are planning to leave," Roger said, as soon as she turned and shook his hand as well. "Tonight. Martin here insisted that we take you along."

Her eyes grew big, and Martin realized he was holding his

breath. Bridget looked around the room, taking in the Kin and the humans.

"And who are you?" she asked the pigs.

"Oh, I'm sorry," Martin blurted. "This is Petunia, and Marilyn, and the red one is Erik."

"Nice to meet you," she said, almost curtsying.

*Strange,* Martin thought. *She might be a little...off. But then, wouldn't anyone be after such an experience?*

"Thank you for asking me," she said, finally. "I will go with you, but I need to return to my room and get my journal first."

"We don't have time," Roger said dismissively.

The woman stiffened and turned on the older man. "I beg your pardon, sir, but I am a writer. I will not leave without my journal."

Martin could see the same doubt about the woman's mental state cross Roger's face.

"Then hurry," Roger said. "We leave in an hour, by the south route. Erik?"

"I told my brother I would relieve him for the evening," Erik said. "We should still have time."

"Thank you," Bridget said. "I'll be right back."

She turned and left before any of them could object further. Erik paused, then hurried after her.

# Chapter Nineteen

Bridget realized right away that the humans and their Kin allies were traitors. She thought about raising the alarm immediately, screaming her head off, but the tunnels were strangely quiet, and she couldn't be sure of anyone hearing her. Besides, she didn't know if the humans were dangerous. They might hurt her to shut her up, or even kill her.

So she decided to play along and look for an opportunity to warn someone.

To her disappointment, they made it all the way back to her room without encountering anyone. She went to her desk and got her journal, then turned to Erik.

"I must have a little privacy," she said, pointing at the chamber pot under her bed.

Erik grunted assent and left the room.

Bridget quickly grabbed her chalkboard and scribbled, "I have been kidnapped by the two humans, Martin and Roger. We are leaving at midnight by the south route. Beware of the traitors: Marilyn, Petunia and Erik."

She looked around for someplace that Blake would be likely to look, and in the end set the chalkboard down on the desk. Then she met Erik at the door.

"I'm ready. Let's go."

The two hills were riddled with tunnels. The north hill was filled mostly with living space for the Kinfolk. The south hill was mostly either space devoted to The Machine or storerooms, with one significant exception: the humans were kept there, away from the Kinfolk.

Erik led the way deeper into the hillside and subterranean corridors until they came to a small exit near the back of the hill. It opened out onto a barren high desert landscape.

They stopped there while Marilyn stuck her snout out of the opening and sniffed.

"What's she doing?" Martin whispered.

"She's seeing if any of the coyotes or ravens are nearby," Petunia said.

"She can do that?"

"We can sense them," Erik answered. "We can control them, the same way we can control the Folk."

Marilyn suddenly went still, and a look of intense concentration came over her face.

*When did I begin to understand their body language and demeanor?* Martin wondered. *I can read them the way I can read other people.*

A coyote had come into view and then had stopped in midstride. It seemed to be shaking, as if fighting for control, and then it relaxed and padded over to them. By then, Erik and Petunia had also taken on that look of concentration, and the coyote curled up by the exit and appeared to go to sleep.

"Hurry," Erik said. "We can only control so many of the lesser Brethren, and only for so long. We must be far from here by morning."

They made good progress at first. The moon was full, and the Kinfolk picked the easiest path through the sagebrush and rocks. But near dawn, they began to slow down. Martin had never been the most physically fit man, and being a prisoner for several years had made him even less so. Roger was both older and injured.

But what really slowed them down was Bridget. Martin saw her stumble into a cactus that was in plain sight right in front of her. From that point on, she had to stop every few dozen yards, complaining the whole time.

The twin hills were still in sight.

Eventually, they reached the lone hill with the wrecked Jeep at its base. There, Bridget insisted on stopping again. Her shins were bleeding, but it didn't look like anything major to Martin.

Suspicion bloomed in his mind. *She's delaying us on purpose*, he thought. *We should leave her.* He almost voiced his suspicions— but he couldn't be sure, and it felt wrong to damn her without proof.

When Erik came up beside him and grunted, "She is malingering. She isn't as hurt as she pretends," Martin was relieved.

"I agree. But what do we do? Leave her?"

"I think we must. I do not believe she wanted to go with us, which means she could have alerted the others somehow. We may already be compromised."

*My fault*, Martin thought. *I insisted she come along, but I forgot how I felt when I first arrived here—I felt welcome and useful.* The Kinfolk had a way of making human misfits part of their circle. He should have known.

Despite the delays, they reached the spot where Roger had parked his SUV as daylight was breaking. He'd told them that if they could get inside, there was a spare set of keys in the glove box.

On top of the SUV was a single raven. Martin noticed the look of concentration come over Erik's face, but instead of the raven freezing as it was taken under control, it cawed loudly and flew away.

"They know," Erik said. At the same moment, a pack of coyotes came around the side of the SUV and blocked their way.

"What do we do?" Martin asked. "Can we fight them?"

"We can try," Petunia said reluctantly. "But if we do, we'd better do so quickly. These coyotes are under Genghis's control, which means he's on his way."

"How did they know?" Marilyn grunted.

Martin turned toward Bridget. "You told them, didn't you? Somehow, you let them know."

She flushed and looked away.

"We'd better do something quick," Roger said. He bent down, picked up a broken tree branch from the sand and hefted it, swinging it around as if to test its weight. Martin grabbed another fallen limb and stripped away the smaller branches. The makeshift club had a satisfying heaviness to it.

Meanwhile, the raven that had flown away returned and landed on the SUV's roof, accompanied by several others.

The three renegade Kin lined up in front of Roger and Martin. There were half a dozen coyotes between them and the vehicle. It looked like an even fight to Martin, but someone was likely to get hurt before it was done.

Surprisingly, it was Petunia who charged first, followed closely by Erik and Marilyn. The Kin were slightly bigger than the coyotes, and their tusks were sharp. Two of the coyotes went flying, while the rest started to snap at the pigs.

Martin swung at one of the coyotes and connected. Its fangs lost their grip on Erik's tough hide, and it rolled to one side. It got up, but it was limping as it attacked again. Beside him, Roger had connected even more solidly. The coyote he knocked off Marilyn's back didn't get up.

And then they reached the SUV. Roger swung at the passenger's-side window, and it shattered. He reached into the glove box and manipulated something attached to the top of the compartment. A set of keys fell into his hand.

"Let's go!" he shouted as he ran toward the driver's side.

No one had been paying any attention to Bridget. She appeared as if from nowhere and met Roger at the door. He didn't see her in time, and she swung the rock in her hand at his head, connecting with a *thunk*. He slid down the side of the SUV and fell to the sand.

Martin hadn't been far behind Roger, and now he shoved the woman as hard as he could. She went flying backward and landed on a pile of rocks. He heard a meaty *thud* and winced. It was both a satisfying and horrifying sound. She didn't move, and Martin saw blood streaming from her head.

Martin was helping a groaning Roger get up and into the vehicle when he felt something tug at his trouser leg and heard the sound of fabric ripping, then a squeal as Erik caught the attacking coyote firmly in the side with his tusks and tossed the animal into the air. It went flying over the SUV, out of sight.

Roger was sitting in the driver's seat, dazed, as if he couldn't remember what to do. Miraculously, he still had the keys in one hand.

"Move over!" Martin shouted, and snatched the keys from the older man. Roger didn't respond, so Martin pushed him toward the passenger seat, harder than he wanted to, but Roger finally got the message and crawled over.

Martin inserted the keys and looked up to see that the three pigs were surrounded by the surviving four coyotes, but seemed to be fending them off.

"You might want to open the doors for us!" Petunia grunted.

Martin realized that they couldn't get in. He lunged over the seat, grabbed at the handle of one of the rear passenger doors, and managed to open it a crack. That's all it took. Erik stuck his snout into the crack and pushed the door the rest of the way open. The three Kin wiggled into the SUV. Once inside, Petunia was able to grab the door handle with her teeth and slam the door shut.

As Martin started the vehicle, he heard a startled shout from Roger and snarling that seemed only inches away. A coyote had lunged partway through the broken passenger's-side window and had a grip on Roger's shoulder. Roger appeared to be too weak to fend it off and was swatting ineffectually at the creature.

Martin swung his fist with all his might at the coyote's muzzle. He felt a flashing pain in his hand when he connected, and a shock ran up his arm, but the coyote let go with a howl and fell backward.

Then Martin was driving away, accelerating as fast as he dared.

He hadn't driven more than a few yards before he realized something was wrong. The vehicle wasn't handling well. It kept pulling to the right. He glanced at the side mirror and saw that a horde of javelinas was running beside the SUV, trying desperately to puncture the tires.

From the drag of the vehicle, it seemed the right front tire was flat.

He kept driving, fighting the constant pull to the right.

A raven struck the windshield, and for a moment all Martin could see was an explosion of black feathers and red blood. Then another raven struck the same spot, and a crack began to appear. Then it was as if an entire flock of them was flying at him, and the crack widened and widened. As the windshield shattered, Martin flinched, and that, plus the drag of the SUV, sent him off the road, into the soft sand.

He tried to keep the vehicle going, but slowly, excruciatingly slowly, it slowed and then stopped, and all he could hear were the tires spinning uselessly in the sand.

Martin had set his makeshift club down beside him, and now he picked it up.

"No," Petunia said. "We must surrender."

"Why?" Martin looked out the window. He spied only three coyotes still moving, and only a couple of battered ravens. "We can still get out of here if I can just get some traction."

They were tantalizingly close to the firm surface of the road. Martin thought if he could get some sagebrush under the tires, it might provide enough traction to get the SUV back on the road.

"Genghis is offering us a deal," Petunia said. "If we surrender now, he won't hurt us."

"How do you know that?"

"Because he just told me…in my head."

Martin turned and stared at Petunia, but she had her head down. In the distance, he saw them coming: dozens of Kin, the larger pigs running among hundreds of the Folk. At the edges of the herd were coyotes, and ravens darkened the sky.

His heart fell. There was no way they could get away.

"I've told him we surrender," Petunia grunted.

As the SUV was surrounded, Martin lay down the club.

"I didn't know you could communicate like that," he said, a feeling of awe running up his spine.

Petunia stared at him, and in her eyes, he saw the same amazement. "Neither did I."

# Chapter Twenty

The GPS coordinates led to the most desolate, out-of-the-way spot in the entire desert. There were few distinguishing geographical characteristics, just mile after mile of scrubland and sagebrush and sand. They were more than 200 miles from anywhere, about as far from civilization as it was possible to get in the modern world.

"The road comes to an end ahead," Enrique told Barry as they approached a hill, standing alone amid the flatness. "We can either debark and go on foot, or risk trying to find a route through the badlands. But if we get stuck, we're screwed."

"How about if we leave two of the vehicles and take two, so we'll have a way to escape if we do get stuck?" Barry suggested.

"Good idea," Enrique said.

They stopped at the base of the hill. A road ran up the side, but they saw no reason to venture up it. They got out and gathered around a map Barry spread out on the hood of one of the SUVs. The map showed few features. The hill in front of them was called El Dedo, The Finger, and there were a couple of hills not much farther on that were called Tetas de Bruja, the Witch's Tits. The satellite data seemed to be pointing directly at that location, but so far, they had yet to see a single javelina, much less a Tusker: plenty of coyotes—an unusual number of coyotes—but no pigs.

Enrique let Harrison get the troops in order while he went off to one side and called his wife. He'd been calling every hour, right on time.

"We'll leave the professor's van and one of the SUVs and continue on," Harrison said.

"No way," Patterson said. "The van goes where I go."

Harrison didn't change expression, and yet an aura of menace seemed to grow around him. "You'll do as I say."

Patterson looked ready to argue, but Enrique returned at that moment and immediately assessed the situation. The two men had clashed from the very beginning. If Harrison wanted to stop for lunch, Patterson wanted to keep going. If Patterson wanted to stop for the night, Harrison thought they should push on. Everyone else followed Harrison's suggestions (or commands), and it was obviously frustrating to the sergeant that this one person felt inclined to argue, and that because he was a civilian, it wasn't as easy for Harrison to order him around.

"It's all soft sand and sharp rock," Enrique pointed out, trying to be reasonable. He knew that he had to back up his sergeant, but was hoping for a compromise.

"And I keep telling you that my van has been modified for just such situations," Patterson replied. "You worry about yourself and your men. I'll take care of myself."

Enrique glared at him for a couple of seconds, then turned to Harrison.

The sergeant looked disgusted, then nodded. "It's your life," he said to Patterson. "But don't say I didn't warn you."

"Yeah, I got it."

This close to their destination, the group decided to travel light, moving most of the supplies out of the Land Rover they were taking into the two they were leaving behind. Half of the men, including Harrison, were assigned to Patterson's van, and the rest piled into the SUV. A couple of men were squeezed into the back compartment, but since they weren't going far, they figured it would be okay. They hadn't bumped along for long before they heard cursing from the back as the men were thrown about as the vehicle lurched over the rough terrain.

It was just barely possible to find a route through the rocks. Often, they had to backtrack, or get out and lift some of the bigger rocks out of the way.

"We could have walked and made about as much progress," Barry muttered.

"Yeah, as long as you're willing to carry an eighty-pound

pack," the soldier next to him said. "Believe me, this is better."

The Witch's Tits were visible almost from the beginning, but they looked closer than they really were, and after several hours, it seemed as though the travelers were no nearer to their destination.

To be fair to everyone, they rotated through the two vehicles, and at one point, Barry found himself in the back of the university van. Patterson had a complete laboratory back there, and it was all packed neatly and tightly to withstand the jolts of rough terrain.

"I've got a souped-up engine, four-wheel drive, fat tires, and six extra inches of clearance, more than the Land Rovers," Patterson announced smugly. And indeed, for every time the van got stuck, the Land Rover got stuck twice, and was harder to push free.

Halfway between The Finger and the Witch's Tits, Enrique called a halt. Sergeant Harrison brought out the map and the two men conferred. Then Harrison folded up the map. "Sir, we're approaching the coordinates with the most javelina activity," he informed Enrique. "I think I should scout ahead. Let me take Holden and check it out."

"What are you afraid of, a bunch of pigs?" Oliver Patterson scoffed.

Enrique turned toward him and said in a mild voice, "You're the one who has been warning us about the mutant pigs, how smart they are."

"Dangerous to civilians, perhaps," Patterson said, then waved at the men around them dressed in camouflage and holding rifles. "But I doubt they'll put up much of a fight against a paramilitary troop."

"Still, it can't do any harm to scout ahead. I don't want anyone to get hurt. So just to be on the safe side..."

"Do whatever you want," Patterson said, getting back in his van. "I'm going on."

None of the other men moved, so Patterson shrugged and started the van.

"Wait," Enrique said. "You can't go alone." He addressed his men. "Holden, Maddux, and McMasters...go with him. Keep your eyes open. We'll be right behind you."

"Yes, sir!" they answered. The farther they went, the more like a military unit Enrique's men were sounding. It was that more than anything that let Barry know they were getting close to the possibility of danger.

As Patterson walked toward the van, everyone's eyes followed him. Everyone saw the ravens at the same time. Even Patterson seemed startled. He stopped and stared up at the birds that covered the roof of his van. The birds weren't moving. They were staring back at him.

It was a moment of eeriness akin to the first time that Barry had looked into Genghis's eyes and seen the malevolent intelligence there. This phenomenon was somehow related, Barry instinctively knew, though he couldn't say how.

Patterson leaned down, picked up a rock, and threw it at the birds. Without a sound, the entire flock of ravens took flight and flew east, the direction the men were traveling.

Patterson got into the driver's seat, started the van, and followed the ravens.

There were too many men left behind to fit in the Land Rover, so Enrique directed some of them to follow on foot, and the rest hurriedly piled in and followed the van. They could barely make out the van's brake lights go on through the cloud of dust it was kicking up, then something came flying out of the cloud and smacked into the front of the SUV.

"What was that?" Barry asked.

"Looked like a dog," one of the men said.

"No," Enrique said, steadily applying the brakes in a way that made the Land Rover shudder but not go off the road. "Coyotes."

Then they all saw them, dozens of the creatures surrounding the vehicle, their lips curled in snarls that the men couldn't hear through the patter of pebbles and sand striking the SUV. As they came to a stop, the animals thudded against the Land Rover in their eagerness to get at the men inside, some rearing up on their hind legs and scratching at the windows, slavering at the men, spraying the windows with saliva.

The dust began to settle around the SUV, and the men inside could see that the university van in front of them had almost driven into a deep ditch that ran across their path, extending out in a gentle curve that seemed to encircle the Witch's Tits, which now loomed over them.

"This ain't normal," one of the soldiers said. "Coyotes don't act this way."

"What do we do?" Barry asked.

"We turn around and get out of here," Enrique said. He was already looking behind him and turning the steering wheel. The coyotes seemed to understand what he was doing and ran toward the back of the vehicle, trying to block the way. Enrique didn't hesitate. He gunned the SUV backward, and it lurched as it ran over several of the creatures. But the others didn't run away. They continued trying to block the way.

As Enrique hit another coyote, the Land Rover slid to one side and smacked against a rock that had been hidden by the mass of animals. There was a grinding sound, like a ship running aground, and the vehicle tilted and nearly went over. When it slammed back down, it wouldn't move forward or backward, no matter how much Enrique gunned the engine.

"Out, on the double," Enrique shouted, grabbing his rifle. He flung his door open so hard that several coyotes were sent sprawling backward, giving Enrique enough room to lower the rifle and start firing.

Barry, on the passenger side, followed his example, and barely lowered the muzzle of his rifle in time to blow away the snapping jaws of the nearest coyote. Flaco was at his side, also firing. Guns started firing behind and across from him as the rest of the men got out.

"Wouldn't we be better off in the Land Rover?" Barry shouted during a lull between waves of attacking coyotes.

"Only if we want to be trapped," Flaco shouted back. "You tell me the Tuskers are the real danger. I'd rather not be spam in a can when they arrive."

"Retreat!" Enrique shouted. The men immediately went into an arrow-like formation, which Barry found himself in the middle of. The back doors of the van flew open, and the three soldiers that Enrique had assigned to it quickly piled out and joined them.

They hadn't gone more than ten paces when the coyotes suddenly retreated as one, as if they'd been given a signal. Enrique started trotting back in the direction they'd come from. The other men followed without question.

"What about Patterson?" Barry asked.

Enrique waved his men on, but he stopped. "Dammit, I knew that man was going to be trouble." He waved Barry on, too. "I'll get him. You stay with the others."

"No," Barry said. "I convinced you to bring him along."

"Follow my orders!" Enrique commanded, sounding completely exasperated.

Just then, the driver's side door of the van opened and Oliver Patterson stepped out. He was fumbling with an odd weapon, and Barry realized it was some kind of dart gun. The professor had refused to take one of the rifles, but he seemed to want some protection now.

"Hurry, Patterson!" Enrique shouted.

Still the professor hesitated, unwilling to leave his precious van. He stared at them, mouth agape, then Barry and Enrique realized that he was staring at something behind them. They turned to see that the men were coming back, the arrow in reverse now, pursued by what looked like a sea of wild pigs.

"Tuskers?" Enrique asked.

"No, these are just javelinas," Barry said. "But the Tuskers must be directing them—along with the coyotes, and probably the ravens too."

"Did you know they could do this?"

"No," Barry said. "When we fought them before, they controlled the javelinas but nothing else."

They heard a door slam, and Barry glanced over his shoulder to see that the professor had gotten back into his van. He was trying to back the van away from the trench.

The rest of the men arrived in a rush, and they put their backs to the SUV and started firing as wave after wave of wild pigs attacked. It was a massacre—none of the pigs were able to get close, thanks to the soldiers' marksmanship.

*What are the Tuskers hoping to accomplish by this slaughter?* Barry wondered.

Then the man beside him swore and searched his fatigues for another clip, finally finding one and inserting it.

"How much ammunition do we have?" Barry asked.

"Not enough," Enrique answered grimly.

Still, they were able to hold their own for a time.

"We have to get back to the other two Rovers," Enrique said as the surviving pigs regrouped for another attack. "We have more ammo there."

"Are you sure?" Barry was liking the secure feeling of having the vehicle at his back.

"Unless you want to fight these creatures off by hand, yes, I'm sure."

Enrique barked a series of commands, and once again, the men got into formation, ready to make a break for it. "We can make it," Enrique said confidently. "If we head in a straight line, we'll move faster than we did in the SUV. We just need to keep breaking the waves of animals. If we shoot the first three or four, the others tend to retreat, so start using single shots. We don't need to kill them all, only keep them from getting near."

With that, the group moved out. They had traveled several hundred yards before the animals realized what they were doing.

Barry glanced over his shoulder at the van but didn't say anything. Patterson had had his chance to join them, but had decided to cower inside his van instead. Barry looked around for Flaco and saw him trailing his son-in-law at the head of the troop.

They heard a huge boom behind them, and a shock wave traveled along the sand like a curling blanket, nearly throwing them off their feet. The Land Rover they'd left behind went flying into the air and landed on its roof, then burst into flames.

The travelers saw what looked like a man pointing a bazooka at them from the defensive ditch that surrounded the Witch's Tits. It took several moments for Barry to realize it was a Tusker, standing on its hind legs. It dropped to all fours and laid the weapon on the ground. Then another Tusker ran up with what looked like a missile and inserted it into the weapon's barrel.

Patterson's van came veering toward them in reverse, then suddenly took off at an angle, heading down a slope to the north and disappearing from view.

Enrique shouted out another series of commands. Barry didn't understand the jargon, but the soldiers instantly obeyed, and the formation veered to the left, to the south. Barry managed to turn with them, bumping up against one of the men.

"Steady on!" the soldier shouted, grabbing Barry's shoulders firmly and pointing him in the right direction.

At the spot the formation would have been if they'd kept running in the same direction, there was a flash, and Barry felt himself being lifted off his feet and doing a somersault. Other men were flying around him, as if they were an acrobatic troupe. It was almost beautiful, and it appeared to Barry as if it was happening in slow motion. Then the sound wave struck, and he couldn't hear anything for a few seconds. He landed flat on his back, then immediately clambered to his feet, amazed he could move at all.

He saw the soldier who had helped him lying nearby and ran over to try to help the man up, but his eyes were empty and dead. Barry looked around and saw that several other men were also lying on the ground, unmoving. Enrique was leaning over one, and turned his head to look at Barry with furious determination. He pointed to the man at Flaco's feet, and Flaco shook his head. He started to walk toward Enrique, then fell over, grabbing his leg. Enrique ran over and lifted his father-in-law onto his back.

"Leave me here, son," Flaco shouted, but Enrique ignored him.

"Come on!" Enrique commanded. "Move it!"

The survivors formed up again and started running.

There was another loud boom behind them, which was frightening, but no further damage was done, and Barry realized they were out of range of the Tusker's weapon.

They turned toward The Finger.

For a few minutes, it looked as though they had escaped. There were no coyotes or wild pigs in sight. They circled The

Finger, all of them running at a steady clip now that they were near the other Land Rover.

But as they neared the hill, they realized that along its base was a solid line of Tuskers.

Barry heard clicking sounds all around him, and looked around to see the soldiers extracting bayonets from their backpacks and affixing them to the barrels of their rifles.

Barry had no bayonet. He hadn't even realized they were used anymore.

"Motivation check!" he heard Enrique shout as they started moving forward again.

"Hooah!" the men answered in unison.

"Moto-mota, got alota moti-vation!"

"Moto-mota, got alota moti-vation," they chorused.

Barry found himself joining in as best he could. It gave him courage, this camaraderie, this union of men.

"Hooah!

"HOOAH!"

And then they reached the hill.

The Tuskers charged.

The two sides met in a clash of tusks versus steel.

It was obvious to Patterson from the start that they were outnumbered and outgunned.

As soon as he saw the Tusker raise the bazooka-like weapon and aim it, Patterson knew that all his theories had been validated. He was right and all his detractors—his mockers— were wrong. A new species had arisen in response to mankind's destruction of the Earth, and it was stronger and faster and smarter than man.

Mankind had had thousands of years of culture to build on to get to this point in its technological evolution. Even so, the majority of humans were idiots. These Tuskers couldn't be much past their first few generations and already they had adapted mankind's technology to their own use. It was a frightening display of intelligence.

Patterson had always hoped that this inevitable development wouldn't be that bad, that it would be manageable, but he'd also prepared for the worst. Now, as the fight seemed to be turning against the humans, he decided he'd learned enough. He had no intention of getting involved in a battle, especially one the humans were losing.

His passengers had leapt out the moment they'd come under attack. Most of them were in a defensive formation near the Land Rover, which was riddled with bullets but still provided the only protection.

The van was being left alone. Patterson put on his seat belt and started the vehicle. He turned the wheels hard to the right and shot off across the landscape, and he felt a strange exhilaration as he dodged rock piles and sagebrush, racing away from the scene of the battle. A few bullets whizzed by, and he heard a couple of sharp clunks, but then he went down a slight incline and was clear of the fight.

The incline steepened, and to Patterson's horror, he saw a steep gully straight ahead. He hadn't even considered such a possibility, the land had looked so flat. He slammed on the brakes, and the van skidded and slowed, but tipped over the edge of the gully, then tumbled down it. His head slammed against the door, dazing him, and then the van started rolling, and his head slammed against the door again, and everything went black.

# Chapter Twenty-One

The soldiers cut a swath through the pigs. Now that they had reached the front lines, Barry saw that it was mostly javelinas, and that the few Tuskers were staying well back. The men lifted the squealing, impaled pigs over their shoulders and shook them off their bayonets, then stabbed others. One of the men, David something, couldn't shake a pig off his blade fast enough, and his vulnerability was quickly taken advantage of. A tusk caught him in each of his legs, and he grunted and fell to his knees, and the javelinas swarmed him.

Barry had stayed back because he didn't have a bayonet. He had a couple of rounds left, though, and he waited for an opening. One of the pigs that had gored David rushed Barry, and he shot it between the eyes. Several other shots rang out down the line, and Barry realized that some of the others still had ammo as well.

Barry lifted his gun and sighted on one of the Tuskers, which was leading its troops from behind. He shot it, and it thudded against a boulder and slid to the ground, leaving a red streak on the rock. At this, about a third of the javelinas seemed to lose heart and went running away from the fight.

The surviving Tuskers took refuge behind the boulder.

Then the men broke through and started trotting smartly over to the two Land Rovers. Enrique had his cellphone to his ear. "Alicia? We're on our way back. What's that?"

Enrique's face went white.

"What did she say?" Barry asked.

"She said, '*They're coming!*' Then the phone went dead."

Sergeant Harrison was starting up one of the vehicles. There was a sudden loud crackling sound, and the man cried out as bolts of electricity shot off the hood and down the length of the car. He managed to get the door open and tumble out onto the desert sand, but he was dead by the time he hit the ground.

Next to him, Enrique bellowed with pain as electric sparks shot out of his phone and into his hair. He dropped the phone and batted at the flames, the scent of singed hair drifting off him.

Other men were crying out too, and as Barry looked around, he saw that all of them were desperately extracting electronic equipment from their belts and packs. Several of them flopped to the ground and started thrashing around.

The sky above lit up brighter than the brightest day as a cobweb of lightning bolts filled the atmosphere from one horizon to the other. The loudest boom Barry had ever heard nearly threw him from his feet, and he cried out and covered his ears.

Then it was over. They sky grew dark; the lightning subsided. Most of the men who had dropped to the ground shakily rose to their feet.

Enrique spoke, and though his voice sounded muted to Barry's ears, he could understand him. The hair over Enrique's ears was completely gone, and his ears were red, but he was otherwise unharmed. "Electromagnetic pulse. Biggest I've ever seen. Any electronics that were turned on are permanently fried." He turned to one of his men. "Try starting the other SUV."

The engine turned over, but immediately began to run down, as if the battery had been drained. At the last second, with some of the men praying out loud, it roared back to life.

The javelinas were circling them but not attacking, and Barry realized that the battle had been about driving the men away, and in that, the Tuskers had succeeded.

Enrique loaded the injured Flaco into the backseat of the functional SUV. Two other men who were too wounded to walk were also loaded in. They'd lost three men in the fight.

Enrique saw Barry standing there, watching. "Get inside the Rover," he commanded. "You're out of ammo, right?"

Barry nodded, but he hated to seek the safety of the vehicle before the others. "I'll wait," he insisted. "I'm not wounded."

"Get in," Enrique insisted. "You'll be one less man to worry about. Get in, dammit!"

Barry opened the SUV's rear door. He glanced to his left as he did and saw wide, churned tracks beside the road, hundreds of hoof prints, and with a sudden chill, he realized that the Tuskers had sent some of their number south. He was certain they were headed for his home valley.

He closed the door and turned to look at Enrique, who was looking back at him with a grim expression.

"I see it, Barry," the staff sergeant said. "We're heading back, on the double."

"How are we going to do that?" Barry asked. "There are too many men to fit into one vehicle."

"You shuttle a group ahead a ways and then come back for the others. Go! We'll be waiting."

Barry got into the driver's seat and waited until the Land Rover was as full of soldiers as it could get: there were even a couple on the roof. But no matter how they crowded in, at least five men would have to be left behind, and then only if they left the water and ammo behind too, and no one wanted to do that. Everyone had reloaded their weapons, but no one was sure it would be enough. The waves of coyotes and javelinas had seemed endless.

Enrique made the decision to leave not five but half of his troops behind, so they would have adequate numbers to defend themselves. This caused a delay, because none of the men wanted to leave. Enrique finally just started pointing at them, one by one, and ordering them to go.

The Rover was sluggish, but Barry finally settled into a thirty-mile-per-hour pace. He didn't dare go faster on the rough road. He hadn't asked Enrique how far ahead he should go, so he decided to drive for one hour, drop the men off, and return.

*How did things get this far?* He had imagined the Tuskers might still be out there, multiplying in number, but despite Lyle's warnings about the Tuskers' intelligence, he had never imagined that they might be organized, that they would develop technology.

He'd thought Jenny was safe in the fortress of the barn. But with the churned-up tracks near the road, heading south, Alicia's last words on Enrique's phone were chilling. *"They're coming!"*

Barry looked down at the speedometer: twenty-eight miles per hour. The SUV was swaying from side to side, sometimes making strange grinding sounds. Behind him, Flaco and the wounded men were moaning from the constant lurching.

He put his foot down on the accelerator.

# Chapter Twenty-Two

When Patterson came back to consciousness, there was silence and darkness. He put his hand to his forehead and felt a lump there, but no blood. His head was surprisingly clear and pain free, as long as he didn't directly touch the contusion. He recalled he had been vaguely aware of guns firing in the background at some point. He must have almost come to before slipping into unconsciousness again.

Miraculously, the van had landed upright. The lab was more or less on an even keel. He turned on the lights; they still functioned. Everything was connected to the van's battery, and he had another as backup. *I should have enough power to complete the job.*

Despite the jolting and rolling, the equipment was mostly intact. Patterson had the latest technology. He replaced his equipment every six months, no matter the cost. The university was happy to let him do it.

He had been extremely lucky to get tenure. Two things had worked in his favor. The first was that the head of the biology department's wife had a crush on him, which he'd swallowed his distaste of and consummated. And his favorite aunt had left him a fortune—after years of making endowments to the university.

He'd been keeping what he knew were heretical ideas to himself, but once he got tenure, he didn't care anymore. He did the bare minimum not to violate the rules of his employment, teaching freshman biology once a year and taking on a few graduate students as assistants. Eventually, those duties had dried up as well. His enthusiasm for teaching had been so minimal that, though the other faculty members couldn't point out anything he was doing wrong, it was obvious he wasn't an effective instructor. And no graduate students wanted to be assigned to him.

That was fine with him. It gave him more time for his own studies.

He'd spend years designing a virus that would specifically target certain DNA markers. All he needed was some fresh DNA, and he'd be ready to reveal his creation to the world. They would have to recognize his brilliance then. But even more importantly, he was convinced he was going to save mankind.

Patterson found the tranquilizer gun still strapped to the backseat and popped it open. It was fully loaded. He went to the back doors and tried to open them, but they wouldn't budge. He crawled over the front seat and tried the driver's-side door, and then the passenger's-side door. With a loud, metallic screech, the latter opened enough for him to get out.

He grunted in pain as he stood up. When he'd been crawling around in the back of the van, he hadn't realized he was hurt. But now, as he straightened up, a sharp pain struck him in his lower back. But after a few steps, he felt himself loosening up, and the pain receded. He stared up the hillside. When he'd been going over the edge, it had looked steep, but now it didn't seem so bad.

He crawled up the rocky incline and poked his head over the edge. The wrecked Land Rover was still burning, glowing red in the night. At first there didn't seem to be anyone around, but then he spotted the outline of a huge pig in the firelight. It was one of the mutants, standing guard, perhaps waiting to see if any humans returned.

He aimed at the Tusker's broad side and fired. The pig jumped and squealed. It ran in a circle for a few seconds, then fell over.

The Tusker's sides were heaving as Patterson carefully approached, as if it was having a hard time breathing. Patterson had used more than the recommended dose, because he didn't have to have a living specimen to extract DNA from. It just made it easier.

Ignoring the glaring red eyes and huffing of the pig, he grabbed it by one of its hind legs and started dragging it back to the van.

He was able to pry open the back doors from the outside. A piece of metal had come off the top of the van and jammed itself into the doorframe. Once he pulled it out, the door popped open.

Patterson dragged the Tusker into the back of the van. It was moving its front legs slightly, so he grabbed a rope and tied its legs securely. He took a syringe full of the beast's blood and got to work.

It would take him at least a day to finish the job.

The column was in full retreat. Barry had always considered it a scouting expedition, but he knew that most of the others had thought they were going on a hunting trip, ready to mow down some sort of animal species that was getting out of control.

Most of the men were quiet, still trying to absorb the incomprehensible fact that they had been defeated, outflanked, and completely routed…by a bunch of pigs. They were down to one vehicle, and it was cramped, with men hanging onto the top and rear of the SUV.

The men left behind kept going on foot, following the Land Rover, but after several attacks, they'd begun taking defensive positions, waiting for the SUV to return. They were barely staying ahead of the pursuing Tuskers.

No one said aloud what they were all thinking, that they were now carrying in two shuttle trips what had taken three vehicles to transport the first time. And they'd left behind the smoldering remains of two big Land Rovers, victims of Tusker firepower and inexplicable science.

The Tuskers knew the terrain, and every time half the group was left behind, there were casualties.

*At this rate*, Barry thought, *it isn't going to be long before we only need one vehicle and one trip.*

Since they could only safely go about thirty miles an hour, they'd settled on shuttling each carload of men an hour down the road before returning to get the others. Thus, their pace was about fifteen miles an hour, sufficient—or so they thought at first—to keep ahead of the pigs. They had at least two hundred miles to go before they reached any kind of civilization. Barry tried to do the math. He knew it was going to take most of the day at least.

None of the cellphones were working. The EMP had fried them.

"Could this be happening everywhere?" Enrique asked.

Barry didn't say what he was thinking—that the Tuskers had shown the ability to disrupt communications before, if only in a single valley. This looked to be a much broader event, though how broad was hard to say.

"What I wouldn't give for some good, old-fashioned, low-tech walkie-talkies," Enrique continued, without waiting for an answer.

The next shuttle trip, Enrique stayed behind with his troops while Barry drove. Barry saw some of the men staring at him resentfully and realized he hadn't taken his turn at staying behind.

"I'll stay this time," he said to Enrique when the next shift happened.

"No," Enrique said adamantly. "You're the boss. You pay us."

"You'll still get paid, don't worry about that."

Enrique looked insulted. "That's not the point. We are trained to take care of civilians...especially the civilians who hire us."

"I'm staying," Barry said stubbornly. "That's all there is to it."

"Okay," Enrique answered. Barry thought he saw a grudging admiration in the soldier's eyes. "We'll take turns staying behind."

Barry knew he'd done the right thing when the men started talking to him again, even deferring to him. Barry suddenly realized that, in their minds, they'd put him second in command behind Enrique, probably because they knew he was paying them, and maybe a little because of his age.

They were following the tracks of the SUV, trying to make

the distance they'd have to cover just a tiny bit shorter.

"Why the hell are we running?" someone asked.

It was Corporal Berger, one of the last-minute recruits to the expedition. With Sergeant Harrison gone, he was officially second in command. Barry almost didn't recognize the man, what with all the dirt and blood on his face.

They were trotting along at a military clip, and Barry was laboring to keep up with the younger men despite not carrying all the gear the soldiers were carrying. He tried to answer through his shortness of breath.

"Because..." huff, huff, "...we're outgunned..." huff, huff, "...and outnumbered."

"You saw that, too, right?" Berger appeared to be in shock. "I didn't just imagine it? A pig fired a bazooka at us, right?"

"You saw it with your own eyes, didn't you?" Barry said.

"But the EMP...that can't be a bunch of pigs. Someone must be behind them. Using them."

Barry turned on him in frustration. "That's your problem, dammit! You...we...underestimated them. That's why we're running. We've been thinking of them as pigs...as brutes. But these Tuskers are something new. They're at least as smart as we are...if not smarter."

The soldier shook his head. Barry guessed that on some level, the man understood the world had profoundly changed, but every other part of him was rejecting it. He'd probably keep on rejecting it until one of the Tuskers got him.

"We're doing this wrong," Berger said. "We should stop and create a defensive perimeter. Running only makes us vulnerable."

Barry thought perhaps that if Enrique was in his right mind, he'd probably agree. But Alicia's words were still reverberating in his ears. *"They're coming."* Barry doubted Enrique would stop for anything.

One of the men in the rear called out, and they stopped and turned. Another wave of Tuskers was coming toward them.

They formed a circle, facing out, and Barry took his place among the soldiers, cradling his rifle. His gun was full of ammunition, so when he saw the wave of pigs coming at them, he didn't hesitate to fire. But after he had dropped three or four of the animals, he realized the others were holding back.

It was only when the wave was less than a hundred feet away that the men started shooting, single shots, making every one of them count. Barry sheepishly followed their example.

It only took a couple of misses for some of the pigs to advance to within a few yards. The men still had their bayonets attached to their rifles, and at this point, they stood up and waited for the rest of the pigs to get close.

It was bloody hand-to-tusk combat after that. The troops still had the greater reach, and in most cases could stave off the pigs' attacks. But Barry saw one mercenary lunge toward a pig and miss. Tusks were tearing into his thighs before he could recover, and he screamed, falling to the ground. The man beside him skewered the pig, but it was too late. The mercenary bled out while another soldier cradled him.

They saw another wave approaching, and just in time, the SUV pulled up. Once again, it was Barry's turn to drive. The troops piled into the vehicle, and Barry ran over a few pigs on their way out. He forced himself to slow down, to avoid the obstacles.

They'd barely paid attention to the rough road into the badlands on their way in, secure in their numbers and firepower. The men had talked excitedly among themselves, eager for action. Now they were silent and grim, fully aware that if their one vehicle broke down on the rocks that lined the middle of the track, they'd be on foot, miles from anywhere, pursued by creatures who were more adapted to the terrain. Barry watched the pedometer and, when he'd traveled the required distance, he dropped the men off and turned around.

When Barry returned, he found Enrique and Berger arguing in front of the troops. It was an astonishing sight, and a sign that discipline was breaking down.

"They're just picking us off one by one!" Berger shouted. "We should be stopping at a defensible position!"

"And then what?" Enrique shouted back. "There's no one coming to our aid! We are on our own! Perhaps we'd be safer in the short run, but what happens when we run out of bullets?

What happens when our enemy keeps increasing in numbers?"

"We don't know that no one's coming," Berger said. "They must be seeing this on satellites."

Barry spoke up. "What if there's nothing that can pick up the signals? What if everything is fried?"

Both soldiers fell silent at this. Enrique recovered first. "I'm giving the orders here, Corporal Berger. Do you intend to follow them?"

They stood only a foot or so apart, leaning toward one another, as if each was willing the other man to back down. Finally, Berger turned away with a snort of disgust. "You're the commander."

Enrique got into the driver's seat. It was Barry's turn to stay behind. He found the camp even more vigilant than usual. They'd lost three men in this round. At first, the soldiers had set up camps in what they thought were defensible positions, the kind they'd used in war. But the animals had used the cover to approach and had overwhelmed them. So they'd started camping in the open, where they could see anything that was coming, and that had seemed to work for a time.

"What happened?" Barry asked in a whisper as Enrique started the Land Rover.

"The men are starting to realize we're running out of ammo. They're becoming stingy with the bullets and waiting too long to fire." Enrique lowered his voice. "Pretty soon, it's going to be every man for himself. I've seen it before."

"We're almost out of the badlands," Barry said. "Another hundred miles. We just have to hang together until then."

Enrique nodded. "I don't understand how the Tuskers are keeping up with us. Even with us shuttling back and forth, there shouldn't be any way they could catch up."

Barry looked up into the sky. A murder of crows was flying overhead in perfect circles, as if the camp below were the bull's-eye of a target. "They aren't keeping up," he said. "They're signaling ahead."

Enrique stared at the circling birds for a long minute. When he finally looked back at Barry, he seemed baffled. "Just how many of these Tuskers are there?"

"More than we ever suspected," Barry said grimly.

Enrique shook his head and drove off.

It was on Barry's next turn in the Land Rover that disaster struck. He'd let one of the other men drive the vehicle because he was worried about Flaco, who was slipping in and out of consciousness. The driver swerved at the sight of three coyotes in the road, and the SUV veered up a lava outcropping and then careened toward the other side of the road. Barry's stomach lurched as they slid into the gully beyond, skewering the oil pan on a jutting rock.

"Oh, God!" The driver sounded panicked. "Oh, God, I'm sorry, guys. I'm so fucking sorry."

"Not your fault," one of the other mercenaries grunted. He turned to Barry. "What do we do now? Go back and join the others?"

They got out and assessed the damage. Barry was stumped by the problem. With enough men, they could probably get the Land Rover off the rock, but they couldn't fix the oil pan and the drive train, which had also been damaged.

"Safety in numbers," one of the men said.

"No," Barry finally answered. "We can't leave the SUV."

They had jettisoned most of the equipment they'd brought along, but they had kept the ammunition and water bottles. Barry estimated that it was still too much for this squad of men to carry, and they would need those supplies. It was bad luck that the wounded were in the camp behind them. They would have to be carried here.

"I'll go back and get the others," Barry said. "I need one of you to go with me."

The troops were silent for a second. "We all volunteer, of course," one of the men said, finally. It was a grudging, subdued admission. "Maybe you just ought to point to one of us."

Barry closed his eyes and pointed over his shoulder. He heard a groan and turned to see that the lucky volunteer was Mark Collins, one of the few mercenaries he'd actually had a conversation with. The man had grown up on a farm and seemed to think he knew all about swine. Barry had tried to convince him that he knew nothing about Tuskers.

They loaded up on ammunition.

"Keep an eye out," Barry warned the others. "They aren't just coming from behind."

The men looked around nervously. "We'll be waiting," one of them said.

As Barry and Collins trotted down the road at a pace Barry never could have maintained only a few months before, he felt a sense of urgency—not just because of his current situation, but because it was clear that the wild pig infestation was bigger and more widespread than he had ever suspected.

And if they were in danger here, what kind of danger where those left behind in? The Tuskers had shown a taste for vengeance, and there was probably no place they wanted to inflict their vengeance upon more than Pederson's barn, where both Flaco and Barry had left their wives and family. It was fortified, sure, but Barry could only hope that those he had left behind were being vigilant.

# Chapter Twenty-Three

Collins and Barry had only gone a few miles before Barry started to lag. He was older than the young soldier by decades. Fortunately, they had traveled only about half the shuttle distance before the breakdown. Otherwise, Barry wasn't sure he could have made it.

It was obvious after a while that he'd made the wrong command decision. He should have sent a couple of the younger soldiers back, and he—old retiree that he was—should have stayed behind. It had always been a problem of his, delegating authority.

Collins could see it too. He was trotting alongside Barry, seemingly without breaking a sweat, while Barry was laboring. Finally, the soldier stopped.

"Come on, we have to keep going," Barry panted.

"No offense, sir, but I could travel faster without you. It's basically the distance of a half-marathon, and I run a couple of those a year. I could get there in a couple of hours."

Barry stopped and bent over, breathing hard. He'd be left alone, and Collins would be alone, with no one to watch either of their backs. But there didn't seem to be any choice. "You're right," he said. "Go on without me. I'll keep going, so we'll meet partway."

"Again, I don't wish to question your commands, sir, but I think you'd better stay right here and rest." The young soldier started stripping down, removing his outer layer of clothing, then handed Barry his backpack after taking a long drink of water. "I'm leaving everything behind except this," he said, slapping the stock of his rifle. "I'll be back soon. Wait here."

He took off running without waiting for a response.

*The arrogance of youth,* Barry thought, and considered trudging onward. Then he decided the young man was right. Better to save his energy for the trip back to the crippled Land Rover.

The hours passed. He saw two jackrabbits, a chipmunk, several hawks, and once, in the distance, he thought he might have seen an antelope. But he was alone, as alone as he'd ever been. It felt good, actually. Barry realized that he'd been craving alone time. He'd become part of something bigger, without ever making the conscious decision to do so. It wasn't like he had any choice. If the Tuskers were as dangerous as Lyle had insisted, Barry owed it to his fellow man to try to stop them. When he'd accepted Lyle's money, he'd made that commitment.

But damned if he didn't wish he could just sit on his back porch with a vodka tonic, play a little pickle ball once in a while, and be the retired duffer he'd expected to be.

One image had changed everything, banished his doubts. He hadn't been surprised when the Tuskers had attacked. But when one of them had risen on its hind legs and lifted the crude bazooka to its shoulder and destroyed the SUV—that had been a sight so astonishing that Barry had known the war he'd feared was at hand.

Who knew what else the Tuskers had accomplished in their last two years of hiding? Who knew how many Tuskers had been born, or how widespread they'd become? He'd heard that the wild pig population in the U.S. had doubled every few years for the last decade. Exponential growth. How many of them were Tuskers? And since Tuskers seemed to be able to control their less evolved brethren (along with coyotes and ravens and who knew what other animals), maybe it didn't matter how many were Tuskers. There were enough to be dangerous. That was becoming more and more clear.

Professor Patterson had seemed like a crackpot, and yet... the evolutionary leap was undeniable. Humans had pushed and stressed the animal populations for thousands of years and finally, nature had responded by creating a species that appeared to be even smarter than humankind. Even more ruthless. In only a few generations, the Tuskers had apparently learned from humans and had begun to adapt. Who knew what they were capable of on their own? Given enough time, was it so impossible that they might eventually outshine humanity?

In one area, at least, they weren't progressing. They seemed as aggressive and vengeful as any human, if not more so.

Perhaps they had more reason to be.

Barry had done research on swine after understanding the danger. He'd seen pictures of female pigs tethered so that they couldn't move, suckling generations of piglets, until they died, still in harness, emptied out. Pigs in stalls so tiny that they couldn't move, pumped full of steroids and antibiotics and fat, sometimes even fed the remains of their own kind.

If humans had suffered such a fate, how would they have reacted if given a chance to rebel? Certainly, human history indicated that they wouldn't have done any better than the Tuskers.

"Perhaps that is up to us," Jenny had said when he'd told her of his musings. "We are the older civilization. Perhaps we should apologize for what we've done and make it up to them. Maybe they wouldn't want to wage war on us then."

"We aren't very good at apologizing," Barry had pointed out. "Not until we've already won. Slavery? Oops, so sorry. Genocide of native populations? Oh, surely we wouldn't do that *now*. Except...I think we would, if we still felt we were being challenged."

"But we have to try—"

"Oh, no doubt. I'm more worried about the human reaction than what the Tuskers might have planned. Lyle wanted us to wipe them out. We took his money because we agreed. But I have to tell you, I'm having a lot of doubts."

"We can walk away," Jenny had said. "I don't need the money."

"Yes, but if we walk away, who will deal with it?"

"We tell the authorities," she'd said. "If they don't believe us, then too bad for them."

"Great, except a lot of innocent people will die before they wake up to the danger," Barry had said gloomily. "What we need is proof."

A black cloud appeared in the sky, interrupting Barry's reminiscing, and he realized it was hundreds of ravens circling something below. Whatever it was, it was fast approaching. Then he saw the vanguard of coyotes, running ahead and beside the troop of humans that slowly came into view.

Barry raised his rifle and looked through the scope. The mercenaries were marching at a good clip, not quite a trot. Three of the men had wounded over their shoulders, and as Barry watched, they stopped and three other men took on the burdens. Collins was leading the way, the only one not carrying a pack.

They reached Barry much quicker than he expected. He rose and shouldered his pack, and held out Collins's pack as the soldier approached. Collins snatched it without stopping, pulling out the water bottle and taking a quick swig, then swinging the pack over his shoulders without breaking stride.

Barry fell in beside Enrique, who was bringing up the rear. "How are the wounded doing?"

"I don't think Shavers is going to make it," Enrique grunted. "Johnson seems okay, though he's not very mobile. I can't tell about Flaco. He isn't conscious very often."

They kept up the steady pace for another couple of miles, then one of the men stumbled and fell to the ground. He sprang up immediately, but Enrique took it as a sign and called for a halt.

It was only after they'd stopped that Barry realized Flaco was moaning loudly. Barry went over to his friend, took out his water bottle, and tried to trickle some water into the wounded man's mouth. Flaco started coughing, but he opened his eyes.

"Leave me here," he muttered.

Enrique had come up behind Barry, and now he crouched beside his father-in-law. "I'm not going to do that, Father."

"You can't give me special treatment," Flaco managed to say.

"I'm not," Enrique said firmly. "I'm treating you the same as I would treat any of my men. I'm not leaving *anyone* behind."

Coyotes surrounded them, and so many ravens were circling overhead that it seemed like a cloudy day despite the clear blue skies. The mercenaries were ignoring them.

Barry caught Enrique's questioning look. "They aren't the danger," he hazarded. "They're just scouts. It's the Tuskers we have to worry about, and wherever these ravens are, the Tuskers aren't far behind."

As if in response, Barry saw the desert wavering, like a mirage. A wave of javelinas was coming toward them. It looked as if the desert itself was heaving, rolling toward them. In the lead were huge Tuskers with massive tusks.

"Time to go, men!" Enrique shouted. They were up and running almost instantly, but as Barry looked over his shoulder, he realized the Tuskers were gaining on them. But instead of attacking the rear guard, the Tuskers ran around them on both sides, until there was a solid circle surrounding the men.

The mercenaries started shooting at the pigs in front of them, trying to open a path, but there always seemed to be more of them. Finally, the men came to a stop and formed a circle of their own, facing outward. They stopped firing, saving their bullets for the final attack.

The largest Tusker in the encircling wave stepped forward. He walked over to where Enrique and Barry were standing, as if understanding they were in charge.

"Surrender," he said, in mumbled but clear English.

Several of the soldiers shouted out in surprise. Barry was rocked back on his heels, barely believing it himself...until the Tusker repeated himself.

"Surrender and live."

Enrique glanced over at Barry. His voice was eerily calm. "Did you know they could do that?"

"Not a clue. Not even a suspicion."

Enrique looked around at his troops. There were only eight men left, not counting the three wounded and the six men who were ahead of them at the disabled SUV. "If we surrender, what happens to us?" he asked the Tusker.

"Sir!" Corporal Berger cried out. "You can't do that." Enrique gave him a stern look, and he fell silent.

"You will be our hostages, for negotiations," the Tusker said. "Genghis wants peace."

Barry didn't believe it, and he could see that Enrique didn't either.

"We will be your prisoners," Enrique snapped, "but we won't allow you to use us as hostages."

The pig shook his head sorrowfully. Barry realized he was completely anthropomorphizing the Tuskers now. And why not? He'd been known to give his cars names and to talk to them. Whether this new species was simply mimicking humans or their behavior was a sign of their intelligence, he couldn't tell.

But he saw that the Tusker wasn't going to take no for an answer, just as clearly as he saw that Enrique wasn't going to say yes. Barry's hand drifted to his belt. One spare clip left. A few bullets left in the clip in the gun. Way too few for the number of creatures surrounding them. He was probably in better shape than the others, because he had had a chance to renew his supply of ammo before he'd left the disabled Land Rover.

Then, as if to emphasize the hopelessness of their situation, he saw more Tuskers coming, a rising cascade of them, even bigger than the group that surrounded them. He glanced at Enrique to see if this new development changed things, but from the grim look on the soldier's face, he saw that they were in for a battle, hopeless or not.

The new wave of pigs didn't slow down, but slammed into the Tuskers surrounding the men. To the surprise of both humans and Tuskers, these new arrivals were attacking their own kind instead of the soldiers. One broke through the circle and ran straight toward Barry. He raised his rifle and started to squeeze the trigger.

"Stop," the Tusker said.

Barry lowered the rifle. The confusion of battle raged all around him, but it was clear that Tuskers were fighting each other.

The Tusker in front of Barry was huge and fat. He looked on the verge of collapse, but his voice was clear. "We are here to help. Take your men and run."

Barry felt someone grip his arm. "This is our chance,"

Enrique said. He pointed to where there was an opening to the west, in the opposite direction from the latest attack. The soldier leaned down and lifted an unconscious Flaco onto his back, shouting orders to his men to retreat. They ran through the narrow opening and away from the Tuskers.

Barry ran as hard as he could, but he was still trailing the others. He glanced back. None of the Tuskers were following them.

# Chapter Twenty-Four

The night turned to day, and then to night, and then to day again before Patterson finished preparing his virus. He'd found a loaf of old bread and a jar of peanut butter in one of the cupboards and made himself a sandwich. He drank a couple of cans of soda, too, which was hot and burning on his tongue but relieved his thirst. Otherwise, he worked on until he was finished.

The last thing he had to figure out was the delivery mechanism. He decided on an aerosol. He couldn't be sure he would get close enough to the Tuskers to deliver the virus any other way. He developed the spray using the water from the van's radiator, and then sat back. It was likely that all it would take would be one dose, though he'd try to make more than that, of course.

He heard a series of grunts from his captive Tusker. The creature had been making sounds like that for hours, but Patterson had ignored them. Now he realized they sounded almost like a language.

It probably was a language...but it didn't matter. He was going to wipe these creatures from existence, talking or not, gun firing or not, intelligent or not. He went over to the pig, the spray bottle in his hands.

"Thirsty?" he mocked, then sprayed the liquid into the pig's face. "And with that, you're dead, and all your kind are dead. Me—one human—has doomed your entire species. So fuck you."

The pig grunted harshly, seeming to return the sentiment, and Patterson laughed.

He suddenly realized he was thirsty and that there was no water for miles and miles. He was probably a dead man, but he'd try to escape if he could, he decided. And if the Tuskers tracked him down, all the better, as long as he had his aerosol in hand.

He went to the pig and loosened the ropes as much as he dared. He couldn't be sure it would escape, but he wasn't about to let the creature loose while he was still around. He would just have to hope the Tusker got away and infected its fellow mutants.

If not, as long as Patterson was alive and had the virus, he would find a way to infect the others.

He pried the van's back door open and hopped down onto the sand. Again, a sharp pain struck him in the lower back, and he hobbled, hunched over, for a few yards before it began to lessen slightly and he was able to straighten up.

He heard a loud caw and turned.

The roof of the van was covered with ravens again, dozens of them, and they were all looking at him. Patterson felt his body go cold, and his heart lurched. He remembered the wave of ravens in the sky during the battle, and the coyotes that attacked alongside the Tuskers, and he was suddenly certain that this mutant outbreak was even worse than he had expected, that not only was one species affected, but so were others, perhaps many others.

It was as if Mother Nature had conspired to create a force strong enough to undo the damage her human children had done to the Earth.

Patterson walked away from the ravens, wondering if they would attack and what he would do if they did. They watched him silently. As he walked south, whenever he looked up at the sky, there was at least one black bird above him or following him, and he knew that he was being tracked.

*Let them find me*, he thought, clutching his spray bottle. *It will give me a chance to make sure they are all infected.*

He found himself surprisingly fatalistic. It almost didn't matter anymore if he survived. His entire existence, from the moment he'd had the insight about his theory, had been directed toward this day. He'd never married, never had kids, and never made many friends. No one would miss him. But he would have done them all a favor, all the humans he'd never met. They would find his research, his unpublished papers, and they'd know that Doctor Oliver Patterson had saved them all.

Flaco wasn't really aware of all that was happening; he just knew it was bad. He was lying on the ground. He opened his eyes and saw that his son-in-law was sprawled nearby, pale from fatigue. Flaco had a vague memory of being carried. Then he remembered being surrounded by Tuskers. One of them had spoken to the men. *That can't be right*, Flaco thought. *I must have been dreaming it.*

Somehow they had escaped the trap. The Tuskers were nowhere to be seen. But even through his overwhelming pain, which made everything else seem unimportant, Flaco understood they were still in trouble.

"Let's go, men," Enrique said, rising to his feet. He didn't even look into Flaco's face as he leaned down and lifted Flaco onto his back with a grunt. Flaco felt a sharp surge of pain, as if he was being torn apart, but he managed not to cry out. As Enrique began to trot, the pain grew with every step until a blinding flash burst behind Flaco's closed eyelids and he fell into unconsciousness once more.

He awoke again as he was dropped to the ground. He cried out.

"I'm sorry, Father," Enrique said, leaning over him. "My strength gave out. Forgive me."

Enrique looked nearly dead. The bones of his face seem to protrude from his skin. Dark bruises surrounded his eyes. The muscles in his cheeks and forehead were twitching.

"Leave me behind," Flaco managed to say again.

Enrique didn't even answer. He was getting to his feet. Flaco saw that they had made it to the crippled SUV just as night was falling. The men stripped the vehicle of supplies, filling their backpacks with food, water, and ammunition. When they were ready to go, Enrique was standing at the edge of the clearing looking east.

"I don't think they're following," he said. "I think we can risk stopping for awhile."

The men nearly collapsed in relief. Enrique had to shout orders twice to get a couple of them back on their feet and on guard duty. "I'll spell you shortly," Enrique assured them.

The men grumbled, which was something Flaco hadn't seen before. The mercenaries seemed very loyal to his son-in-law, and Flaco was proud of that fact. But Corporal Berger's objections to retreating were starting to have an effect. Now that he wasn't being jostled about, the pain was receding enough for rational thought.

He was lying between two other wounded men. Peter Sterns was the least hurt, and while Flaco lay there, eyes closed, he heard Enrique approach and ask Peter if he thought he could move on his own.

"My legs still work," Peter said. "I'll go as far as I can."

"Good man."

Flaco kept his eyes shut, because a thought had come to him, and he was certain that if Enrique looked into his eyes, his intention would be clear. But Enrique instead leaned over the other wounded soldier, who was so injured that Flaco couldn't even recognize him.

"Hang in there, buddy," Enrique said softly.

Flaco didn't open his eyes until everyone else was gathered around the campfire, which they had built up high. The sagebrush was dry but burned quickly, and they were constantly adding to it. The fire would scarcely flare up with new fuel before quickly dying down again.

Some of the soldiers were sleeping, but others were gathered around the fire, staring at it silently. Tomorrow they would either find transportation, or they would fight their final battle.

It grew darker and colder. Flaco had been drowsing, but he awoke with a start. Something was different. It took him several minutes to figure out that it wasn't a noise that had woken him, but the absence of noise. The gravely wounded soldier had stopped breathing.

The other wounded soldier, Peter, was no longer beside him, but standing near the fire, leaning on a makeshift crutch.

Flaco was alone.

It took every bit of energy he possessed to begin crawling, but he found that the farther into the darkness he went, the more determined he became. He actually rose to his feet and staggered for a distance. He felt rock under his feet, and it was easier to walk on than the sand. It would also obscure his tracks. He kept going, past the point of pain, past consciousness, as if he had turned into some kind of zombie.

Suddenly, a fear arose in him that that was exactly what had happened. He was dead, walking even though he was nothing but a corpse. He fell to his knees and, in a panic, clamped his fingers over his wrist. There it was: a fluttering, swift, weak pulse, but a pulse nevertheless.

He got up and kept going.

# Chapter Twenty-Five

"Are you all right?"

Jenny, who had thought she was alone, cried out in alarm at the voice behind her.

"Sorry." Alicia Morales had poked her head through the trapdoor of the crow's nest, and now she came the rest of the way through.

"I'm fine," Jenny said.

"It's just that you're spending all your time up here," Alicia said, sitting in the lawn chair next to Jenny. The telescope was still bobbing from Jenny having let go of it.

"I'm...just being careful. I thought I saw...something."

"Something?"

"I thought I saw a Tusker. But I can't be sure. So...well, you weren't here, Alicia. You can't imagine how terrifying it was."

"My imagination is good," Alicia said. "Especially when it comes to Felix's safety. What should we do?"

"Have you target practiced today?"

Alicia scrunched up her small, delicate face, and her wide brown eyes showed doubt. "I don't like it. I don't like guns."

"I know you don't, but for Felix's sake you have to take it seriously," Jenny said.

"Is that why you allowed these men to stay?" Alicia asked. She sounded faintly judgmental.

The "City Commission" as they called themselves—though their activities looked more social than business to Jenny—had stayed late, drinking hard, and at the last minute, Jenny had asked them if they wanted to stay over.

To her surprise, when the men had woken up that morning,

having camped out on the floor in some of the Army surplus sleeping bags Barry had stockpiled, they had seemed to be in no hurry to leave. Three of them were middle-aged and single, with former spouses and kids who lived far away. Only Jerry Olsen had family in town, and after breakfast, as he was leaving, he'd paused in the doorway. "Jenny, I'd...uh...I'd like to show Sherry and the boys your ranch," he had said hesitantly. "It's very impressive. Do you mind if I come back this afternoon?"

Apparently, Jenny wasn't the only one sensing danger. "Of course," she'd said. "I'd love to meet them."

Olsen had seemed grateful, and had taken her hand in his. "We'll be back as soon as I can round them up."

Loud bangs from below interrupted Jenny's musings on the morning's events, and she managed to restrain a start of surprise. She was getting used to the constant firing of rifles.

"Those men wanted to try the automatics," Alicia said during a break in the firing. She got up and closed the trapdoor, muffling the noise enough for them to continue their conversation without shouting.

"Flaco wants to leave town again," Alicia said. "Maybe go to New York this time."

"I don't blame him," Jenny said. "It's probably a good idea."

Alicia slumped in her chair. "I'm scared, but I don't want to leave. Are you sure those...creatures are coming back?"

"Barry is certain. I wasn't so sure, but...well, like I said, I saw something strange the other day. And have you noticed all the ravens hanging around? That seems like a Poe-sized ill omen."

As if to accentuate her comment, a fluttering shadow fell over them, and a cloud of ravens flew overhead. They landed on the trees at the edge of the nearby pasture, filling every branch and then some, the overflow landing on the fence.

Jenny had an urge to go downstairs and turn on the electricity in that fence, which had been shut off when they'd sold the last of the cattle.

"That's creepy," Alicia said.

Perhaps if the ravens hadn't drawn their attention, Jenny wouldn't have seen them.

She grabbed the telescope and swung it around, barely

missing Alicia's head. She landed on the Tuskers on the first try. There were five of them leading a host of javelinas, and...Jenny felt a cold chill as she saw the coyotes lined up behind them.

"Go downstairs," Jenny said, grabbing the rifle that was leaning against the railing. "Tell the others to get ready."

Alicia rose without a word, threw open the trapdoor, and stood on the top step of the metal spiral staircase. She pulled out her phone and punched in the number. "Enrique," Jenny heard her say. "They're coming!"

Then she cried out, and there was a clatter as the phone fell from her hand and tumbled down the stairs. The lights in the barn flickered, then went out.

Cassius felt as if he was coming home—which was nonsense. He hadn't even been born during the first battle for Genesis Valley, and yet...it felt familiar. Science couldn't account for this kind of familiarity, he knew; but then, science couldn't account for the Kin's quantum leap in intelligence, nor for their telepathic ability to communicate with ravens and coyotes. And perhaps other animals as well. Perhaps it was only that those two species had been conveniently nearby and easy to control.

Cassius had even heard rumors that Genghis could communicate with some of his followers directly, over a distance, though he'd never experienced that himself. He was proud that Genghis had chosen him to lead the assault. Brutus, his lieutenant, obviously felt it should have been him.

Cassius had chosen to call himself what the human called him. It tickled Cassius's pride to use the Roman name, for it wouldn't be long before the Kinfolk conquered the world, just as the Romans had.

The lights going out in the barn was the signal. The giant machine that Tesla had built in the hill had been activated. If it had worked properly, any human machine with hundreds, perhaps thousands of miles, had ceased to function. It was possible, according to Tesla, that the entire world grid had been disrupted, though he hadn't guaranteed it.

Cassius began to marshal his troops, coyotes in front to act as the shock wave. He didn't really care if they were wiped out.

They were constantly fighting his control, and it was wearing him down. The ravens were a little easier, but weren't much use beyond intelligence gathering.

From them, Cassius knew there were two soldiers, three civilian men, two women, and one child inside the barn. He was also aware that they were heavily armed. He looked up at the crow's nest and saw a flash—a reflection from the telescope. Any chance of surprise was gone.

It would have been better to get into position in darkness and surprise the humans at first light, but Cassius was anxious to get it over with. He didn't think the humans would be able to put up much of a fight once their defenses were breached.

"Should we wait for the gas?" Brutus asked. They had run ahead of the crew that was carrying the containers of sleeping gas.

"We aren't using the gas."

"But Genghis said..."

"Genghis isn't here," Cassius snapped. "Think of it, Brutus! The events of this day will be recounted for as long as the Kinfolk have history. We will be legends, famous throughout time. We will be glorious conquerors."

"Only if we win," Brutus said. He was usually gloomy, which was probably why he was a lieutenant, not a commander.

"But what glory is there in using gas that simply puts our opponents to sleep? How would that tale be told? No, better we win in battle, and win where the First Ones could not."

"You think you're better than the First Ones?" Brutus exclaimed, scandalized. "You think you can succeed where First Father failed?"

"Of course not," Cassius said. "It is in his honor that we must attack, not simply put our foes to sleep." Actually, Cassius *did* believe his generation was better than the First Ones. First Father had operated as much from instinct as from knowledge. Despite his giant intellect, he'd made the mistake of underestimating the enemy. But Cassius and his fellow second-generation Tuskers had the advantage of having been taught by a human, of understanding the humans' psychology, and of being taught all about human history, all the battles and wars.

Most subjects had bored Cassius, but he'd been entranced by war. He was damned if he was going to let this opportunity pass by.

He heard distant guns, and knew that the cadres of javelinas he'd sent into the town were starting to attack. But he wasn't worried about the rest of the valley. The real enemy, the humans who had ultimately defeated First Father, was inside the barn.

The javelinas that were carrying the explosives had arrived. That's what he'd been waiting for. He waved the coyotes forward and took a position from which he could observe the action.

Jenny ran down the stairs to check on the others.

Barry had built portholes all along the sides of the barn, and the men had already positioned themselves there. Alicia designated herself ammunition supplier, after she made sure Felix was hidden behind a wall of supplies.

Barry had warned Jenny not to be overconfident, and yet… what could the animals do? The barn was reinforced on all sides, they had impressive firepower, loads of ammunition, and luckily, with the inclusion of the men of the city commission, enough people to man the defenses.

She pulled Bart aside. "There's a generator at the south end of the barn. See if you can't get it started."

She grabbed as many clips of ammo as she could carry and ran back up the staircase. She heard the roar of the generator as she was closing the trapdoor, and the lights went on. She turned just in time to see the first wave of coyotes swirling toward them. Behind them, she saw two Tuskers watching and realized that they were the leaders.

She raised her rifle and shot in their direction, purposely firing high over them, aware that at this distance she had little chance of hitting them. To her surprised gratification, one of the javelinas near the Tuskers went down, all four legs splaying out from under it. The Tuskers quickly took shelter behind some nearby trees.

*Good*, Jenny thought. They would have less visibility to command their troops. She emptied another clip in their direction, just because she could and because it felt good. She didn't hit anything that time, though.

As if in response, she saw the ravens rise up out of the trees and fly as a sold black cloud in her direction. She fired at them, sending black feathers and torn bodies spewing from the wave of birds. Then they were almost upon her, and she realized she had no real defense against them. She grabbed the rifle and sprang for the trapdoor, scrambling down from the crow's nest, slamming the door behind her and latching it.

There was a series of loud thumps, as if the ravens were throwing themselves with the full force of their wings against the solid wood of the door.

These creatures were under the control of the Tuskers, Jenny saw clearly. They weren't attacking in suicide waves of their own accord. *If I can somehow kill the Tuskers who are controlling them, most of our attackers will probably slink or fly away*, she thought.

But the Tuskers hadn't looked as if they were going to expose themselves, not when they had lesser creatures at their command.

Something about the Tuskers' bearing struck her. They had looked strangely martial, like generals. She crouched on the steps of the staircase and waited until the thumping of falling ravens stopped. She counted to ten, then got to her feet before she could change her mind and threw the trapdoor open.

There were no ravens on the platform. They were swirling about overhead, but it took them a few moments to notice her and respond—just enough time for her to stand tall, raise her rifle overhead, and shout at the top of her lungs, "Come and get us, you cowards! Quit hiding behind your followers!"

Cassius couldn't hear what the woman was screaming, but the challenge was unmistakable. It was as if she was reading his mind. What would history say? That he had led from behind?

"What are you doing?" Brutus cried when Cassius stepped out from behind the tree.

"I'm going to lead," Cassius said, "as I was meant to. Stay behind if you like, Brutus. I'll be sure to mention it in my reports."

The firing from the barn was steady now. The scene was chaotic. The coyotes were darting around, the javelinas were running about mindlessly in packs, and throughout it all, the ravens swooped and circled.

The woman had once again been driven from the crow's nest. Cassius was free to do what he needed to do without being observed.

It was exactly as they had planned: let the humans be distracted by those who couldn't really harm them, while those who could came ever closer. Cassius motioned for the two Tuskers carrying the explosives to follow him. He directed the bulk of the javelinas and coyotes away from him, leaving only enough of the creatures in front of him to obscure his approach.

Then he started forward, steadily, with the same motion as the rest of the attackers, scrambling from side to side, but always moving forward. One of the explosives-laden Tuskers was shot down in front of him, and Cassius snatched up the bundle of explosives with one tusk and continued.

They reached the side of the barn, and Cassius breathed easy for a moment. The humans couldn't reach him from the portholes, so it was safe to drop the satchel and root around in it until he found the mechanical gloves and donned them.

The other Tusker, who was an explosives expert, was already setting the charges. Cassius watched him and tried to copy him, but in the end, the underling examined his work, then grunted and rearranged the wires to his liking.

Then he nodded to Cassius and sprang away. Cassius followed, then realized, as they reached the middle of the yard, that in their haste to escape the explosion, they had made the mistake of running in a straight line.

He felt something hammer into his left side and found himself sliding across the ground, his tusks digging into the soil and throwing him upside down. He tried to rise and collapsed. He realized his back left leg was hanging on by a thread, and then the pain struck, and with it came a clear thought: *I acted vainglorious, just like a human. I was contemptuous of them, and yet I emulated them.*

Another bullet thudded into his side, and he couldn't

breathe. As he flickered in and out of consciousness, he thought, *Brutus was right. We should have just gassed them.*

As he slipped into unconsciousness for the last time, he heard the explosion and felt it lift him from the ground, and he knew peace.

The Kinfolk would remember him.

Brutus didn't like Cassius. The Kin beat him at every test—not definitively, that would have been endurable, but only by a fraction, and in ways that were open to interpretation. Brutus knew himself to be more cautious than his commander, and he'd been instructed by Genghis to let Cassius take all the chances, but to make sure the job was done.

Well, Cassius had done as expected, and Brutus found himself admiring his commander's foolhardy courage despite himself.

Now it was his turn.

The two Tuskers with the gas containers had arrived. They'd been slower because the canisters were bigger and heavier than the explosives. Now everything was in place. There was a giant gash in one side of the barn. The coyotes and javelinas were attacking, but the humans were defending the opening with all their firepower.

But Brutus didn't have to get that close. He only needed a clear shot.

He loaded the bazooka-like weapon he'd carried all the way from Utah with one of the canisters. He'd have two tries. It would only take one of them to do the job.

He raised himself up on his hind legs. Of all the things he'd trained for, this had been the hardest. Learning to remain upright and steady at the same time had required hours of practice.

He took a deep breath and pulled the trigger.

For the second time, Jenny dared to open the trapdoor. The ravens were waiting for her, but she had fashioned a club out of some broken lumber and started swinging, smacking feathered bodies left and right. But there always seemed to be more, and eventually she threw up her arms to protect her face and took a quick look into the yard.

The explosion had completely surprised her. Despite all they knew about the Tuskers' intelligence, she didn't think anyone had expected them to master explosives.

Now, even more alarmingly, she saw a Tusker rise up in the middle of the yard and point a huge weapon at them.

There was a puff of smoke, and a shining projectile whizzed toward the barn. She heard it clunk against the structure's side. A cloud of smoke arose, drifting out over the yard, and wherever the white cloud went, javelinas and coyotes dropped in their tracks.

Uncertain anyone below could hear her, she screamed, "Don't let it shoot again!"

Then Jenny raised her rifle and took aim.

The Tusker had reloaded and was rising up on its hind legs again. She fired into its body and saw it stumble, then out of sheer willpower, for it was bleeding in multiple spots, the Tusker steadied itself and took aim once more.

The missile flew.

Jenny heard it clatter across the concrete floor of the barn. A whiff of smoke reached her, and she grew dizzy. She scrambled to the trapdoor and closed it just as she fell over.

Fortunately, the smoke had the same effect on the ravens, for her arms fell away from her face, and she lay there helpless.

Jenny awoke with a monster at her throat. She cried out at the enormous eyes and long snout, and reached up to strike at it.

A human voice emerged from the horror. "Careful, Mrs. Hunter. There's still gas in the air."

Her eyes focused and she saw that it was one of the soldiers, Serge, wearing a gas mask. His image was wavering because she too was wearing a mask, and the plastic in the eyeholes wasn't clear, making it seem as though she as underwater.

"Fortunately, it seems that your husband thought of everything," Serge said. "Even gas masks."

"Mr. Pederson," she gasped.

"Pardon?"

"Lyle Pederson thought of everything," she said. "Barry and I only inherited it."

"Well, all I got to say is, it's a good thing he was so paranoid."

Jenny sat up. She was inside the barn. Serge had managed to carry her down the staircase. She looked around. Everyone was wearing a mask except Bart Hoskins, who was crumpled on the floor. Serge caught her glance.

"I didn't get to him in time, and I'm just letting him sleep. We were short one gas mask anyway."

Jenny felt a sudden sense of panic as she realized she had no idea how much time had passed or what was happening outside. She staggered to her feet and weaved toward the stairs. She grabbed the metal rails and started pulling herself upward. Serge followed her, making concerned sounds, but she ignored him. By the time she made it to the top, her head was clearer. She shoved open the trapdoor and crawled out on the deck.

The yard was full of dead or sleeping pigs and coyotes. She almost breathed a sigh of relief, then saw the row of animals lined up on the ridge. There were only a dozen or so of them, but they looked like creatures out of myth. It took her a moment, but then she realized that the long snouts and huge eyes of the creatures were, in fact, gas masks that had been constructed to fit the faces of pigs.

*Where are you, Barry?* Even behind the high, strong walls of the Pederson farm, she felt vulnerable. She could only imagine what Barry and the rest of the expedition might have run into.

"Come down," Serge urged. "You need to eat, and to rest."

"No," she said. "I'm not leaving until my husband returns."

The soldier stood there helplessly for a few moments, then turned to go. "I'll bring some food up," he said. Jenny barely heard him.

# Chapter Twenty-Six

After the disappearance of his father-in-law in the dark of night, Enrique was frantic to find him. At daybreak, he sent his men out in every direction, but they found nothing. Not even Flaco's footprints.

Finally, Barry pulled him aside. "Flaco made his choice. He knew what he was doing."

"But we're so close to getting help," Enrique blurted. It was the first time Barry had ever seen him lose control. "There's a town just ahead!"

"He's *gone*," Barry said gently.

Enrique looked around and realized his troops were scattered across the landscape. If they were attacked now, they would be defenseless. Corporal Berger was standing to one side, glaring at him. Some of the men were clustered around Enrique's subordinate, as if they were looking to Berger for leadership instead of Enrique.

"You've got a duty to your men," Barry insisted.

Enrique blanched, realizing he'd been acting like a son, not a commander. He didn't want to return to Alicia without being able to tell her that he'd done everything he could to find her father. But Barry was right. Flaco had made a conscious choice to sacrifice himself, and in that, Enrique could find some pride. But if any of his men were hurt while he pursued a selfish agenda— that he couldn't live with.

"Suspend the search," he called out. "Fall in!"

They continued their march. They had to stop several times to fight off groups of Tuskers, with casualties each time. If they'd had to carry Flaco, there might have been more skirmishes. In his heart, Enrique knew that Flaco had done the right thing, what any good soldier would have done.

*But how am I going to explain that to Alicia?*

They saw the market from miles away, the only building in the entire town lit up by electricity. On the map, the small town was called Lakeside. Enrique had never heard of it, and there was no lake in sight.

When they arrived, they found most of the residents congregated in the market, which had a generator rigged up. Enrique commandeered an Escalade from one of the patrons, who objected until Enrique pointed his gun in the man's general direction and told him he was taking the vehicle.

He tried his best to warn those inside of the approaching danger. He could tell they didn't believe him, and was tempted to stay and try to convince them, but again Alicia's words came to him: *"They're coming!"* He shook his head and left the store. He'd done his best. They were on their own.

Enrique pushed the red button on the key fob, and the large black Escalade beeped. The men started to pile in, and Enrique saw, both to his relief and his sorrow, that they were so diminished in numbers that they'd all fit into the vehicle.

The Escalade sped down the nearly deserted Utah and Arizona highways. They'd be home soon, now that they had real roads and transportation again. Distances that had taken hours to cross earlier on were now traveled in minutes.

*Hang on, Alicia.*

Patterson could see the tracks of the retreating men, though they were almost obliterated by the hundreds of coyote and javelina prints. He came across the bodies of two soldiers, but that was all. Most of them had apparently gotten away.

Patterson refused to think about the odds against him. He had no food or water, the other vehicles were probably gone, and the enemy, who had eyes on the ground and in the air, surrounded him.

By some miracle, he reached the road. There had been a great battle here, obviously, and he found the torn-up body of another man. There were two shredded tires lying there, but no vehicles.

Patterson started down the road.

He hadn't gone far when he saw a lone coyote staring at him from the middle of the road. It trotted insolently away, and for a few minutes, Patterson dared to hope the animal had free will, that it wasn't being controlled. And then the ravens began circling over his head like so many vultures, and he knew he'd been found.

He kept going. What choice did he have?

His hand was sweating on the spray bottle. He was going to make sure he infected more of the creatures before he went down.

On a slight incline, he saw a welcoming committee. To his dismay, there was only one Tusker, and it was staying well back. It was the coyotes that were there to meet him. He charged them, and he felt them tear at his legs, but he was somehow lucky enough to break through and get within a few feet of the Tusker.

Patterson sprayed and sprayed, filling the air with the solution, praying that a few drops would reach the creature.

Then he was on his back, and a coyote had clamped down on one of his arms. He let go of the bottle with a frustrated cry. Another coyote had its jaws only inches from his face, snarling madly, saliva dripping down onto Patterson's chin, its eyes both furious and strangely detached, as if the real coyote beneath the control was simply puzzled by what was happening to it.

Patterson waited for the final lunge.

It didn't come.

The coyotes retreated, and Patterson sat up. The Tusker was regarding him from inches away.

"Come," it said clearly.

All resistance went out of Patterson when he heard that. He staggered to his feet. He was surrounded. The Tusker started walking back toward the twin hills.

Patterson followed. The bottle had broken and it contents had soaked his clothing. He now had one hope left: that he could get close enough to another Tusker to touch it.

All of Patterson's worst suspicions were confirmed as they

approached the Witch's Tits. It was an entire city, concealed from the world, with working electrical lights and machine-tooled tunnels. He passed rooms filled with supplies, and other rooms where Tuskers were obviously being taught.

Things appeared to be in a bit of an uproar. The pigs had been found, and it looked as if they were scrambling to move.

The only question Patterson really had was, why was he still alive?

They brought him to a throne room. Patterson couldn't think of anything else to call it. It was bigger than the other chambers, and at the end was a raised dais, and on top of the platform stood the single largest Tusker Patterson had yet seen. It had hair hanging down its face that looked like a Fu Manchu mustache, and Patterson realized that this was the leader Barry had called Genghis, the last of the first generation and the progenitor of all the remaining Tuskers.

*Too bad we couldn't have killed this one before he spread his kind.* But perhaps...perhaps he could deprive the Tuskers of his leadership, if only he could get close enough.

There was a human woman sitting next to the Tusker, and at a loud grunt from Genghis, she rose and addressed him.

"The Great One wishes to know if you are Oliver Patterson, professor of biology at the University of Oregon."

"I am," Patterson said, amazed.

"The Great One says that he has read all your papers and congratulates you on the confirmation of your theory."

*Am I supposed to say thank you?* Patterson wondered. And yet, he did feel proud of his accomplishment. Word would get out eventually. Especially if his virus worked. Especially if mankind survived this titanic shift in evolution.

"Humans had their time, and they abused it," the woman said, obviously translating the series of grunts and snorts from the giant Tusker. "They have created their own doom through their cruelties. We, the Tuskers, have arisen to take their place, to once again shepherd nature and take care of it."

Patterson shook his head. "You don't seem any better than us humans," he said. "You kill just as readily."

"No," the woman translated. "We defend ourselves, and by

defending ourselves, we are defending all Earth's creatures."

"When you're the dominant species, you will be no different."

The grunt was loud and final. The woman jumped a little at the forcefulness of it. "No. We will not follow your example. To prove it, I must tell you a story."

There was a long series of grunts, and the woman listened carefully, screwing her face up in concentration. Then she said, "As you have probably surmised, we have not arisen from wild javelinas. No, First Mother was raised on a human farm. They called it a farm, but it was a factory. She was held in a stall barely bigger than herself, and she was repeatedly impregnated. But she was lucky compared to some.

"The terrible truth was, she was probably not the first of our kind to have self-awareness. There had already been generations in her family who fully understood the horror of what was being inflicted upon them. They were trapped, unable to communicate their intelligence—and if any of their keepers suspected, they kept it to themselves.

"Somewhere in our past is a mother who was tied into a booth, her legs spread in the air, and she gave her milk to litter after litter of our kind, some of whom were like us, intelligent, most of whom were not, and almost none of whom were her own children. She was milked like that until there was nothing left, and then she died. Gratefully. Free at last.

"My father, whom the humans called Razorback, was perhaps another jump in evolution. He realized he could control the Folk. And he fathered his first litter and planned his revenge. My father was without a doubt intelligent, but he was filled with hate, and he instilled that hate in me and my brothers and sisters. He didn't think beyond killing as many humans as he could, and that led to our downfall.

"But I escaped. I understood we could not win, that we would be hunted down and killed...or worse, captured and tortured to find out what made us tick. So I became determined to make sure that the Kinfolk would survive, no matter what. I have sent my people everywhere I could, generation after generation of them. If this enclave is destroyed, others will take its place. In time, our superior intellect will allow us to find a way to survive the humans, and even to defeat them. And when we win this struggle, we will not treat the lesser creatures as mankind did. This I promise."

The Tusker had become more worked up the longer he spoke. His followers were hanging on his every word. Patterson saw his chance.

He'd been rubbing his hands over his shirt and pants, hoping that some of the fluid that had dried there would transfer to his palms. The virus was designed to work with very little contact.

He leapt forward. Halfway to Genghis, he felt his heart soar, knowing that he was going to destroy this arrogant creature and all his kind.

But then the Tuskers surrounding Genghis surged forward and blocked his way. He screamed as he was hauled backward. At the same time, he ran his hands over his captors' snouts, slicing his hands on their tusks, knowing their saliva would activate the virus.

He fell backward, and one of the Tuskers loomed over him. The animal was furious, and he heard grunts in the background as the pig lowered his tusks, catching Patterson under the chin. The pig reared his head back, and Patterson heard his skin rip and saw the spray of blood like a cloud over his eyes. Only then did he feel the pain.

He closed his eyes against the stinging blood and felt his body grow weak. He smiled. He was not the only one who was going to die. With his death, he was saving mankind. He was killing off an entire upstart species. It was, strangely, enough.

"Why is he smiling?" Bridget said aloud, not really expecting an answer.

"Take him away," the Great One grunted. "Do not eat him. There is something wrong with him."

One of the Tuskers grabbed the dead man by an ankle and started dragging him away. Another Tusker grabbed the other ankle, and a red smear was spread across the throne room as the body was removed. Other Tuskers came out of the shadows and mopped away the evidence of Patterson's demise.

"Prepare to leave," the Great One said, addressing his followers. "I want everyone out of here by tomorrow evening."

Bridget hadn't intended to speak, but she'd been wondering something. "What are you going to do to the other humans?"

The Great One stared at her for a long time, then shook his head. "We can't take them with us. And we can't let them go."

"Oh," Bridget said in a small voice.

"But you will come with me, Bridget," the Tusker said. "You will safe with me. I need your help."

"Of course," Bridget said, her concern for her fellow humans vanishing under a wave of pride. "I'll be glad to."

# Chapter Twenty-Seven

Jenny Hunter waited for her husband to return. She was camped in the crow's nest, refusing to go inside. The others would bring up food and water, and occasionally keep her company, but eventually she was always left alone, as she preferred.

They had barely survived the siege of Pederson's farm, despite being heavily fortified and well supplied. She shuddered to think what dangers Barry and the others might have run into. It was clear that the Tuskers were far more organized than they'd thought.

She could see a band of Tuskers on the slight hill at the edge of the property. These animals had not joined in the attack, but had sent the lesser creatures: the javelinas, the coyotes, the ravens. As she watched, the biggest of the Tuskers rose on his back hooves and seemed to look directly at her. The pig had his gas mask pushed up, so that from a distance, it looked like a tricorn hat.

She shivered. The Tusker's posture was so confident, so arrogant. Despite having been thwarted so far, the leader of the Tuskers didn't seem at all discouraged.

*He looks like Wellington,* Jenny thought. *Looking out over his army.*

She'd lifted her gas mask a couple of times and taken a sniff. She couldn't be sure the sleeping gas was gone, because she hadn't smelled it the first time. Now, she looked through the telescope and realized that like their leader, the surviving Tuskers had taken off their masks. She decided she could risk removing hers. The damn thing was getting itchy and smelly.

As night fell, the floodlights came on, powered by the

generator. Lyle Pederson had thought of everything. *If he'd just stayed inside his fortress, he might be alive today,* Jenny thought. They had provisions and ammunition and all the fuel they needed for the generator. They were as safe as anyone could be.

She watched the line of pigs with their outlandish gas masks, wondering what they were planning next. As if in response, she saw a wave of creatures surge over the hill toward the barn. The Tuskers weren't finished with them yet.

At the same moment, she saw a huge black Escalade come barreling down the highway toward them and turn into the long driveway. Then the attackers were upon them.

To Barry's relief, the single road into Saguaro was still accessible. Maybe the Tuskers hadn't gotten there yet.

Then he saw the explosion in the distance, and even from far away, it rattled the Escalade's windows. He knew instantly that the detonation had been at the barn. They were already driving fast, but after the blast, they tore down the country roads and reached the Pederson ranch in minutes.

There were pig, coyote, and raven bodies strewn everywhere.

Piled up against the sides of the barn were hundreds of javelinas and Tuskers, most shattered by explosions and gunfire, but many still heaving against the reinforced sides of the barn as though their sheer weight would break through.

In places, the reinforcing planks had been torn off the sides of the barn. The pigs were using their tusks to cut into the wood, and some of the holes were almost big enough for the animals to get through.

The guns sticking out of the apertures were still firing, but the attackers were now too close for the openings to be effective. Amidst his alarm, Barry felt relief flow through him so powerfully that he could barely hold up his rifle. There were survivors in the barn.

With that thought, his strength returned, and he raised his rifle and shot at the pig nearest the largest gap in the barn. All around him, the other men were firing, too. The attackers were breaking off their assault on the barn and turning to face them.

*Good*, Barry thought. *Let them come. Let them face a real army.*

On the small hillside above the barn, he saw Tuskers gathered together. They were a weird sight in the billowing white smoke that was wafting through the yard. They looked as though they were wearing masks. As Barry watched, one of them fired a canister of some kind at them. It hit the ground and started to smoke. Part of the cloud reached the men, and Barry suddenly felt dizzy.

"Gas masks!" Enrique shouted, and to Barry's amazement, the troops pulled small metal canisters from their packs, no bigger than a can of deodorant, out of which they extracted flimsy masks that nevertheless hugged their faces and apparently kept them from breathing the fumes.

Barry didn't have one of those handy packs out of which the men could miraculously pull bayonets and gas masks and God knew what else. He felt himself getting sleepy, and heard himself say, as if from a distance, "Shit."

When he came to, he sensed that he'd only been out for a few minutes. Barry felt something covering his face. He realized groggily that he was wearing a gas mask and that the eye slits were out of alignment, so he quickly adjusted them. Enrique was looking down at him.

"You good?"

"I think so," Barry moaned. The aches and pains in the rest of his body were almost enough to drown out the pounding pain in his head. "What's happened?"

"We've driven the creatures away," Enrique said. "They didn't put up much of a fight. I think there was only one Tusker alive, guiding the javelinas and coyotes. He set off an explosion of some kind of gas and got away. He apparently decided the better part of valor was to live to fight another day."

"Jenny," Barry said, groaning as he sat up. He'd been sprawled in the back seat of the Escalade. All its doors were open. There were bodies lined up outside the doors of the barn. His heard sank when he saw Jenny among them.

"She's OK, I think," Enrique said. "She gave you her mask, even though she knew it would put her to sleep. It was a sleeping gas, not poison. I think we'll fully recover."

Barry walked over to the line of recuperating humans. At first, he didn't recognize the extra men. Then he saw that it was the "Zoning Committee."

*How did they get here?* Barry wondered. But since each of them had a rifle in his hands, he was grateful. He nodded to them.

Jenny was starting to stir. He hurried to her side. He looked back and saw that the soldiers were starting to take off their masks, so he slid his down around his neck, leaned down, and hugged Jenny just as she was sitting up.

"Did we win?" she asked.

"We're alive," he answered. "We made it just in time."

"Thank God," she said, raising her arms. He leaned down and helped her to her feet. She buried her head in his shoulder, crying.

"Where's Papa?"

Jenny let go of him reluctantly and they both turned.

Alicia was standing in front of her husband, but pushing him away, looking up into his face and seeing the truth.

"Enrique!" she cried. "Where's Papa!"

# Chapter Twenty-Eight

The prisoners were led to a storeroom in the very center of the hill, surrounded by the bustling activity of Tuskers removing the supplies from the storage rooms in preparation for the evacuation of the entire complex.

"What are they going to do to us?" Martin asked.

None of the others answered, but in their silence, Martin had his answer—the same conclusion that he had come up with. The Tuskers couldn't let them go, nor were they likely to take the humans with them to wherever they fled.

"We are traitors in their eyes," Petunia said sadly. "We will not be allowed to spread our heresy."

So they sat, waiting for the end.

After a day or so, the door opened. The prisoners retreated to the back of the room, as if that would do them any good. But the door slammed shut again almost immediately, and they realized that someone had been hauled in and left there. It had taken four Tuskers to drag Goliath's unconscious body into the storeroom.

They surrounded the Tusker, and Erik leaned down and sniffed him.

"Is he...is he dead?" Martin asked.

"No," Erik said. "I think he was gassed by Roger's sleeping gas. He should wake up just fine."

Goliath arose a few hours later, shaking his massive body as if trying to shake off the effects of the gas.

"How did they catch you?" Marilyn asked.

"I started asking about what happened to you," Goliath said. "Apparently, Genghis already had suspicions about me, and my questions confirmed them. Last thing I remember was going to sleep in my room."

And with that, their last hope died. They had no further allies outside their prison doors.

During their first day of captivity, they'd been given meals, but soon after Goliath's arrival, it grew strangely quiet outside. There was no more banging around, no sounds of footsteps in the corridor.

"Are they all gone?" Petunia asked. "Did they just leave us here?"

"One way of dealing with the problem," Roger said. "But a very cruel one."

Martin realized that he hadn't translated Petunia's grunts but the older man had still answered her. He asked, "Are you understanding them now?"

Roger shrugged. "I got the gist of it."

"I don't believe that even Genghis would do such a thing," Erik said. "There's something wrong."

That evening, after hours of not hearing anything outside, they decided they had to try to escape.

"If we could only get the door open," Marilyn said.

"This wasn't meant to be a jail cell," Erik replied. "It was being surrounded by Kinfolk that was really meant to contain us. If there is no one watching, I believe we can get out of here."

They started opening boxes, looking for something to pry the door open or pick the lock with. After a few minutes, Roger said, "Wow."

"What is it?" Martin asked.

"This box contains things I had at the cabin," he said. "What are they doing here?"

Erik walked over, raised himself up on his hind legs, and looked in the box. "The Kinfolk raided every building within reach. It certainly is lucky that your stuff is in this storage room."

"What do you have in there?" Martin also looked into the box. It was full of knickknacks: picture frames, books, a couple of old wristwatches and wallets, sports cards, pencils and pens, string and wire, and other things that most people would have thrown out.

"Bunch of junk," Roger muttered. "God only knows why I saved this stuff."

He rummaged around some more and finally pulled out a long piece of thin metal. "Anyone know how to pick a lock?"

Martin shrugged. "How hard can it be?"

Half an hour later, he was cursing. He would feel the lock mechanism begin to move, and then the wire would slip and he'd hear the works click back into place. He stood up and threw the metal "key" against the door. "Screw it."

"Let me try," Roger said. He bent down, and within minutes was muttering to himself.

"Any other ideas?" Marilyn asked, after another hour. They'd given up trying to pick the lock and hadn't found anything strong enough to make much progress against the solid door. By design or bad luck, the supplies in the room were mostly soft goods.

"I think the hardest thing in this room is my head," Roger said in frustration. "And if I don't get something to drink pretty soon, I'll be tempted to bash it against that door."

"Well, that's one way to escape," Petunia said.

They gave up for a time, all of them staring at the door as if that would somehow open it. Then they heard the bar across the outside of the door being lifted and dropped to the floor. There was a click as the lock was turned, and the door opened.

They stood facing the door. Erik appeared ready to charge at whoever came in, but Goliath grunted at him and he stood still.

Whatever they were expecting, it wasn't a single human woman.

Bridget looked the worse for wear. Her hair was straggly, her once-firm, abundant skin was sagging. Her eyes looked desolate. "They're all gone," she whined. "The Kinfolk are gone."

"What do you mean?" Goliath said. "They left you here?'

"No!" she wailed. "They're *dead*!"

Petunia rushed to the door, then had second thoughts. "What do you suppose happened?"

Roger gently led the woman into the room. He turned her

around to face him. "What happened, woman? Tell us what you saw."

"They started getting sick," she said. "Like they had the flu or something. Coughing and hacking, just like...just like humans. It was terrible. I couldn't do anything for them."

"All of them?" Martin asked. "They're all dead?"

"Yes!" she shouted. "How many times do I have to tell you? They're all dead!"

The Tuskers and the humans exchanged glances, uncertain. Goliath rumbled, "We'll leave here, but don't touch anything. Stay away from the bodies."

"It doesn't seem to affect humans," Roger said. "I'll get some water and food to bring along."

"No, don't touch anything. Let us leave this place."

They encountered the first Tusker body just outside the door, their guard, no doubt. Before long, they were finding bodies everywhere. They had to step carefully over some of them, squeeze by others. Goliath didn't have to repeat his warning about not touching them. Bridget followed them meekly, and no one stopped her.

"No javelinas," Martin said after they had made their way out of the inner warrens.

"They probably ran off once they were no longer controlled," Marilyn said.

"Didn't you feel anything?" Roger asked curiously. "I thought you Tuskers could read each other's minds."

"I certainly can't," Marilyn answered. "But yes...I felt something. But I thought was only my own dread."

"Me too," Erik added. "I almost said something, but figured that I was just scared."

They reached the entrance and stopped, mouths agape at the scene that greeted them there. As if being in the open would somehow cure them, most of the Tuskers had gone outside. But they hadn't made it very far. Some of them were on their backs, others were sprawled, legs akimbo, headfirst in the dirt. Most of them had vomited. They had fluid coming out of their eyes and snouts.

"Where do we go?" Petunia said, her voice forlorn.

"My cabin is within walking distance," Roger said. "I have a well, with fresh water. Hopefully they left some food."

"Too close," Goliath muttered.

"You have any better ideas?" Roger retorted.

They stood there for a few more moments, hesitant to leave the tunnels.

"Ready?" Roger asked the others, finally. They turned to Goliath for confirmation, and he grunted assent.

They hadn't gone very far before they saw one of the Tuskers at the edge of the clearing struggling to stand up.

They stopped and watched. The massive Tusker finally got to its feet and shook its head.

It was Genghis. He turned his red eyes upon them, and the sight of them appeared to rejuvenate him. "*You*," he said, his voice weak but growing stronger with every word. "You brought this disease here."

"We did not," Roger said. "You managed to do that by yourself."

The pig started tromping toward them, his hooves slamming into the ground emphatically, as if he was coming back to life with every step.

"Stop there," Goliath said, moving in front of the others. "You are finished, Genghis. Let us go."

"Not as long as I'm alive," Genghis answered. "No human will be allowed to live. Stand aside, Goliath. I have no argument with you."

"Humans and Tuskers will have to live together," Goliath said. "If you had been a wise leader, you would have seen that. You made the same mistake as First Father. You underestimated the humans."

"Underestimated?" Genghis said, stopping several yards from them. "I have no doubt the humans are the cause of this plague. I never underestimated their evil. It is you, Goliath, who fails to see that the humans will never allow us to survive. Stand aside."

"You will have to fight me to get at them," Goliath said.

"So be it," Genghis said.

"Please stop!" Bridget said, rushing forward to stand before the Tusker leader. "We can be friends. I'm proof of that. We can work together."

Before anyone could react, Genghis lunged forward. His huge tusks flashed upward, catching the human in the thigh, and Bridget let out a soft cry as her femoral artery was pierced and blood bloomed on her leg, quickly soaking her trousers in a dark rush.

"I don't need you anymore," the Tusker said as he tossed her to one side. She fell limply, her eyes wide open, staring into the sky. Then she turned her head, her breath huffing dust into the air, and then went still.

The humans and Tuskers facing Genghis backed away—all but Goliath.

The two Tuskers faced each other, one of them with blood dripping from his tusks. Seeing them this close together, Martin realized that Genghis was even bigger than Goliath. He'd always seen Genghis from a slight distance, surrounded by his guards. He had never really understood how giant the Tusker leader was.

The two charged each other. They slammed into one another, tusk to tusk, and there was a screeching sound as their tusks clashed. Goliath was pushed back a few inches, and when they broke apart, it was apparent that each had taken the other's measure and that Genghis had gained confidence, while Goliath was suddenly cautious.

Again they charged, and again Goliath lost a couple of inches. As the fight continued, he was slowly pushed back. The humans and Tuskers retreated with him, until they had once again reached the opening to the tunnels.

Genghis seemed to have gained renewed vigor, while Goliath was hanging his head in exhaustion.

"Should we help him?" Martin asked. "Why aren't we helping him?"

"No," Goliath grunted. "This must be done by one of his own."

Martin wondered why. There were no witnesses. No one cared. It only mattered that they escape.

He looked over at Erik, and it was as if they were thinking

the same thing. As Goliath was pushed back against the wall, Erik rushed forward, flanking the larger Tusker, and cut into Genghis's flank. Goliath surged forward at the same moment, and for the first time, it was Genghis who was pushed back. He was bleeding from one side. Erik had continued to circle, and now he came in from the other direction.

In a whirling movement too fast to track, the massive pig met his charge and hurled the smaller animal into the air, spraying blood. Erik landed with a thud and lay unmoving.

Martin saw that Marilyn and Petunia were gathering themselves to spring forward, and that Roger had found a branch to use as a club. But before they could act, Goliath renewed his attack, and with each charge, Genghis was forced to retreat.

They stopped where they had started, and now it was Goliath who appeared invigorated and Genghis who was thrown into doubt.

The giant pig suddenly heaved, and a greenish-yellow fluid spewed from his snout. Everyone stared at the stinking puddle. Genghis was sick. He was weakened from loss of fluids.

Goliath shook his head and charged, but instead of meeting his opponent head on, he turned slightly and raked Genghis along his side. Something began to protrude from the gaping hole, glistening wet, and then giant pig's intestines spewed out onto the ground. Genghis followed them, landing with a wet splat. He grunted once or twice, and then vomited again, the yellow bile mixing with the visceral fluids that surrounded him.

Goliath stood over him, sides heaving, and watched as his opponent died.

Petunia and Marilyn rushed to Erik's side. They sat on their haunches and stared down sorrowfully.

"He's dead?" Martin asked. They didn't answer, but he knew it was true.

Goliath shook himself and turned. Martin expected him to be angry at their interference, but Erik's death had changed things.

"Even sick, Genghis was stronger than me," he grunted. "I wish..." He shook his head and turned away.

They left Pigstown behind, not looking back.

# Epilogue

As darkness fell over Pigstown, deep in the hillside, Professor Oliver Patterson awoke. He didn't know he was Oliver Patterson, or that he had been a professor. He didn't know he'd been alive, or that he'd been human, or that he'd died. He only knew that he was hungry.

He got to his feet, and his brain sluggishly reactivated his sense of balance and mobility. He lurched forward until a door confronted him. He bumped against the door, once, twice, then stood there for long minutes, no real thoughts entering his decaying brain, but the urge, the hunger, still drove him, and out of the dim recesses of his memories—murky, unclear, and confusing images—his automatic motor skills reached out his hands, and he lifted the latch.

He entered the hallway and walked instinctively down the corridor. He stumbled over something in the darkness and fell hard, his skull cracking against rock. He smelled the rotting body of another creature nearby. He tore into the dead Tusker, chewing on the tough skin until he reached the soft flesh beneath, and then ate his fill.

He felt the body of the Tusker begin to move, and as the pig got unsteadily to its feet, the thing that had been Oliver Patterson lost interest in it. Together, the two creatures stumbled down the hallway, eating from those who had not yet reanimated, joining those who were stirring. They weren't awake, exactly, or even alive, but they were mobile, and they were hungry, and they had instincts and dim memories.

They reached the outside eventually, stumbling, running into walls, tripping over bodies. There, they ate the dead until they regurgitated their meals, and then they ate again, and slowly, the bodies they were feeding upon roused and joined them in eating those who had not yet reanimated.

The giant pig near the entrance to the tunnels rose last, half eaten but still imposing. It no longer had a long mustache to identify it, but still retained an instinct for leadership. It groaned, and the others stopped what they were doing and stared with dim eyes at the first one among them to make a sound.

Nearby, a smaller pig arose. It had been a mortal enemy of the bigger Tusker, but it didn't remember this. It didn't remember that it had died to save its friends. It only knew that it was hungry.

A human female also arose, standing near the others, her entrails dragging along the ground.

As a group, followed by all the other dead creatures, they followed the leader, who had once been called Genghis.

He led them toward the living, whom he could sense even from the middle of the desert. He led them toward the valley where he had been born, and where he had nearly died, and to which he now instinctively longed to return.

# About the Author

D uncan grew up and spent most of his life in Central Oregon, the dry side of the Cascades, and whose terrain is featured in many of his books. He wrote several books out of college, including the heroic fantasy novels Star Axe, Snowcastles, and Icetowers. In 1984, he and his wife Linda bought Pegasus Books in downtown Bend, Oregon, which they still own and operate. They also ran a used bookstore, the Bookmark, for 15 years.

In the last five years, he's been able to get back to writing again, and found that he has a lot of pent-up creative energy. He's written numerous books for several different publishers, mostly in the horror or dark fantasy genres, though recently has been branching out into fantasy again, as well as thrillers.

Curious about other Crossroad Press books?
Stop by our site:
http://store.crossroadpress.com
We offer quality writing
in digital, audio, and print formats.

Enter the code FIRSTBOOK
to get 20% off your first order from our store!
Stop by today!